BROKEN EGG

## ALSO BY RAYMOND DOWNING

*The Wedding Goes On Without Us, including Bury Me Naked*

*As They See It: The Development of the African AIDS Discourse*

*Suffering and Healing in America: An American Doctor's
View from the Outside*

*Death and Life in America: Biblical Healing and Biomedicine*

*Biohealth: Beyond Medicalization, Imposing Health*

*Global Health Means Listening*

*Such a Time of It They Had: Global Health Pioneers in Africa*

# Broken Egg

Raymond Downing

Published by Manqa Books
www.manqa.net

Editing by Keith Miller
Cover and book design by Edward Miller
Cover photo by v2osk (adapted)
Inset cover photo by Raymond Downing
Copy editing by Edward Miller

First Edition
10 9 8 7 6 5

To Jan

MANCHESTER CITY
18 94
GOOD NEWS
WE REPAIR
BROKEN EGGS
MANCHESTER CITY

# BROKEN EGG

*Kenya, sometime after the post-election violence (January 2008), but before Kenya's invasion of Somalia (October 2011)*

# Somalia

THEY EMERGED FROM the tent bone-tired: Mlongo first, ducking to fit through the doorway, then Linda, a foot shorter and two decades older, and finally the translator. The tent, white and ribbed, was like half a gigantic oil drum on its side. Mlongo's blue shirt had dark half-moons of sweat at the armpits; Linda's white top stuck to her back, outlining her bra straps.

"So." Linda turned to Mlongo. "This is the last interview?"

Before Mlongo could answer, two teenage boys greeted them in fractured English. "Welcome to Dadaab! How is you? From what country?" they asked Linda. "Come. We sell leather—real leather."

One of them put a wallet in Linda's hand. She ran her thumb over the smooth, shiny surface and handed it back. Mlongo said he was sure the leather was real, but he didn't have money with him. Maybe next time. But the boys were insistent, like *matatu* touts trying to herd customers into their vehicle.

The translator seemed to have disappeared. Mlongo and Linda were propelled behind some tents, where they found two other teenage boys holding AK-47s. Linda seized Mlongo's arm and turned, but the boys stepped in front of them, rifles raised. Linda's mouth was suddenly parched. "We have to go now," she told them, but the boys shook their heads.

The two without rifles hooked arms with Mlongo and Linda, and walked them forward as if they were all lifelong friends. She could hear the footsteps of the gun-toting boys behind. In two minutes they were out of the Ifo camp. There the two guards with AKs pushed them into the back of a pickup idling behind some small acacias. The guards jumped in with them, and the truck sped away. When they were out of sight of Ifo, the pickup slowed and one guard handcuffed Mlongo's right ankle to Linda's left. The captives sat with their backs to the cab, spines jolting against the metal.

For over an hour the truck bounced over sandy tracks, weaving between acacia bushes and small trees. Linda and Mlongo sat in silence, averting their eyes from their captors. Linda felt dizzy, her heart pounding. Suddenly, the guards burst into jubilation. Linda and Mlongo looked at them inquiringly. "Somalia," one guard said. "We reach Somalia!" There had been no fence, no gate, no border post.

They drove ten or fifteen more minutes, then came to a small town. Most of the dwellings were traditional Somali homes, round structures covered by mats or skins. The pickup slowed as it

approached the center of town: three brick buildings with dozens of young men outside them, most
armed, wearing red-and-white-checked keffiyehs on
their heads.

More jubilation: like fishermen returning with
a catch, graduates coming home with a diploma,
hunters coming in with a kill. They had succeeded,
and the attention was on the driver and guards more
than on Linda and Mlongo. The captives shuffled
awkwardly to the rear of the pickup, arms around
each other, and then sat. On Mlongo's count of
three, they hopped to the ground. Their guard kept
his rifle pointed at them as they struggled to keep
their balance. Using the muzzle of the rifle, he prod-
ded them into one of the brick buildings, through
the front room and into the back: an empty room
with one small, high window. The guard retreated,
and they heard a key snicker in the lock.

It was now dusk, and the room had no other
light. Mlongo and Linda sat on the cement floor.
They had said nothing during the ride in the pickup;
conversation came no easier now that it was quieter
and they were alone. Linda still felt dizzy, and now
couldn't catch her breath. She took her pulse: quite
a bit above one hundred, she guessed. She began
her own differential diagnosis: pulmonary embolis?
Myocardial infarct? It was, briefly, an effective way
to deny that she was terrified.

She licked the dust from her lips; she felt intense thirst. Then her first response medical training kicked in: "Well, Mlongo, it looks like we've been captured, or kidnapped, or something. What should we do?"

"I was about to ask you the same," he said. "We'll get out—somehow."

"You mean try to escape?"

"No…I mean we're not the first health workers kidnapped, and most of them eventually get released. It's just that it could take a while."

"Will there be a ransom or something?"

"Yes, I hear there often is." Now the diplomatic role: "Of course, we don't really know why we've been captured, or what these folks want. Or even who they are. I guess it's too early to try to figure this out."

"Yeah," Linda said. Yeah, we don't know. Just something else we don't know. Yeah, this messes up our trip. Yeah, it messes up what I was trying to do at the District Hospital too. Yeah, and we can barely talk to these guys—I hope they have a translator.

She put her head back against the wall and closed her eyes. Somewhere a goat bleated. She could smell woodsmoke.

After an hour or so one of the guards brought in two bowls of rice and lentils, and a flask of water. He stood by the doorway, one sandaled foot up on the wall, watching while they ate. When they had finished he brought in two foam mattresses, pointed to them, and then went to the doorway and sat. Mlongo said in Swahili he wanted to know where the latrines were. The guard went out again. He came back with a second guard, who removed the cuffs from their ankles and took Mlongo out while the first guard stayed with Linda. When Mlongo returned, the guard took Linda out.

*

This procedure was repeated every evening after dark: two bowls of food, two mattresses, an escorted trip to the latrine, and a guard with a lantern sitting in the doorway all night.

The days had only a little more variety. There were no attempts at religious or political indoctrination, no threats, no torture. They either sat in the room with a guard, or out in the back, chained to an acacia tree. Food came twice a day, midmorning and after dark. They were given no clothes except what they had on; whenever they bathed, they washed those clothes, wrapping themselves in a blanket while the clothes dried.

After the first day of what would become a monotonous schedule, Linda and Mlongo found huge blocks of time to fill. There were no patients to see, no meetings to attend, no decisions, no crises, no news. And underneath, the fear that was always there.

"Well," Mlongo said on the second day, "I wonder what's next." They were sitting outside on white plastic chairs, chained by the ankle to the acacia tree. It wasn't yet noon, but it was already hot, and the acacia provided only a ragged shade.

Linda had slept poorly and now had a headache. "Gee, I don't know. Isn't this when they tell the news media and ask for a ransom?"

"Yeah, maybe." Mlongo rapidly bounced his knee.

Linda moved her chair slightly to get under a scrap of shade. The flies that had been circling her head followed her and she swatted at them. A rooster crowed. "Do you think there's anything we can do?"

"Huh? Oh, no, of course not."

*

Mlongo's foot was still on the accelerator even though his vehicle was in neutral, and it took some time for him to release it. But he did release, after several days, and eventually he would just sit, composed, drawing serenity from a source deeper than he could name.

Linda, on the other hand, had a slow fuse, slow enough that most people never knew it was lit. She relied on that fuse for the first week, and it served her well. She was patient. Her patience was real, not just an act, in the same way her fuse was real. But sometime in the second week her apparent equanimity began to erode.

"Mlongo, could you please stop humming that tune? I'm tired of it." It was something she might have said to her husband, Bill, but never to a coworker.

"Sure." No tune.

Then, a minute later: "Oh, I'm sorry, Mlongo. We've got nothing else to do here. Go ahead and hum if you want."

He smiled, but didn't hum.

Linda's worst times were at night; raw fear kept her awake. She created detailed scenarios of how her children, Josh and Angie, would handle her not coming home. And more detailed scenarios of how she would die trying to escape, or as she was being rescued. Oddest of all was the guilt—the same guilt some women feel after they've been raped.

One afternoon, chained to the acacia, Mlongo suddenly broke his silence. "You know, Linda, we shouldn't have done that last interview. We were both tired, and it was too close to the edge of the camp."

"Yeah, but it never occurred to us that we'd be kidnapped! And besides, you asked how I was doing, and I told you I was fine for another interview."

"Well, it should have occurred to us. I mean, lots of Somalis have been kidnapped by Shabaab…"

Before she could stop herself, Linda interrupted, "But not expat aid workers!"

Mlongo fished in his pocket for his handkerchief and wiped the sweat from his face.

Linda's neck turned red, but not from the heat. "I…I meant aid workers," she said. "From anywhere."

Mlongo kept wiping. With something that might have been a smile, he said, "Well, it is true that I'm not Somali."

# The Doctors

*One Year Earlier*

## 1

WHY DO MONDAYS have to be so annoying? If she had only slept well. Robin chats made a racket in the trees right outside her bedroom window. Linda had assumed it was dawn, but the luminous dial on her clock read three twenty-six. Pitch black outside. What's wrong with those birds? Now I'll never get back to sleep, and I'll lose three hours. She jerked onto her side, yanked up the pillow, and slammed it over her head. Stupid birds!

It felt like she had just gotten back to sleep when she heard the robin chats again, and now the roosters were having their morning shouting fest, each waving his noisy flag from his own compound. She grumbled and checked the clock again: six eleven. OK. She pulled aside the corner of the curtain: now there was the pink glow. The compound guard was slouched in his chair in the guard shelter, legs stretched out, wrapped in a long coat, hat over his eyes. Perfectly still. Perfectly asleep.

OK, might as well get up, pee, put the coffee on, feed the cat…put one foot in front of the other as she had done every morning for—what, was it already ten years? Maybe not quite. Now that she lived alone there were few new events, and no other people, to challenge the routines. Or habits. Or maybe ruts. The coffee was on, its rich aroma starting to fill the house; the cat was fed. She combed her grey hair in front of the paperback-sized mirror on a shelf—the only mirror in the house—and fastened it in the same ponytail she had worn for close to forty years. Her clothes too were functional: patterns that didn't show stains easily, plenty of pockets. And, for these last ten years, trousers instead of skirts.

She sat in her chair next to the table lamp with the old-fashioned shade and read the daily readings, then prayed. Or was it meditating…or maybe just drifting.

She made breakfast: black coffee, toast with jam, and yogurt. The same every day, the default jam being red-plum Zesta since she could no longer find mulberry on the supermarket shelves. It was a good part of every day: work hadn't intruded yet, and she was fortified by the warmth of coffee, the sweet crunch of toast, the cool yogurt.

Monday morning. Mercy comes today to clean. Mercy Onyango, who she had known for twenty years, who had started with them as their housemaid when the children were young. She had come every day back then, washing the dishes, cleaning the house, cooking sometimes, watching the children when she and Bill were busy. Besides being the organizer of all domestic tasks, Mercy was also their first Kenyan friend. They practiced Swahili with her, they used her as a window into village life…and they paid her. Was that friendship? Who were her friends now? Mercy certainly—but they hardly saw each other because the hospital was so consuming.

OK, might as well leave the breakfast dishes for Mercy and get going. She stepped outside to begin her walk to the District Hospital, and again it was the weather that reminded her that days carry no grudges. She tasted the air itself—the taste of a tall glass of cool water. The sky beyond the big eucalyptus trees was celebrating the color blue, blessing the green trees and brown path. Two tiny children in school uniforms walked past, arms around each other's shoulders. Down the lane a young man in shorts was stomping in a shallow pit of fresh mud; his companion was packing the mud into the brick mold, then turning the wet bricks out onto the ground to dry.

At the T-junction half a dozen young men straddled or stood next to their motorcycles, awaiting passengers. The newspaper salesman thrust the morning *Nation* in front of her, as he did every morning, and she declined with a half smile, as she did every morning. When she turned the corner, a fellow on a bicycle pedaled past, trailing a pungent sweat smell, carrying an old woman seated sidesaddle with a huge basket on her lap. *Matatu* vans honked and jostled for passengers. She threaded her way between them, past the carpenters making sofas, beds, and coffins, past the gigantic empty billboard frame, and on to the hospital.

The front of the hospital was handsome. Linda remembered seeing it for the first time several years earlier, in a PowerPoint presentation of family-planning services. In the slide, two tall, exotic palm trees had stood to the right and left of the front door; manicured hedges ran the length of the hospital; the hospital name above the front door was freshly painted. The sun was shining and the lawn in front of the driveway was freshly trimmed, with visitors sitting serenely on the grass waiting for visiting hours to begin.

That was still the hospital she saw this morning, though she was aware that several windows behind the hedge were broken, the faucet in one of the sinks ran continuously, and the only place fresh paint was evident was the sign over the door.

"Daktari. Daktari Linda." The assistant matron pounced as she walked through the doorway, dodging people who had come to visit their patients. "There is an *mgeni* here for you."

"Good morning. An *mgeni*? A family member of one of the patients?"

"No, no, another *mzungu*. He is from St. Anthony's."

"From the clinic? I didn't know they had any *wazungu* there anymore."

"Come. Come now. He was waiting at my office when I arrived. He has asked two or three times for you. Come…" And she took Linda by the hand and pulled her to her office.

Outside the assistant matron's office a tall, elderly man in a safari suit rose from the bench as Linda, propelled by the assistant matron, rounded the corner. His bushy white eyebrows twitched. "Dr. Linda Jankowski," he said, and extended his hand. "I am Dr. Hans van der Stoeckle from the Netherlands. We discussed already that I am coming to see you early this morning."

Linda shook his hand. "Good morning," she said, and furrowed her brow. "Um…perhaps you could remind me. I'm not sure I remember having an appointment this morning. When did we discuss—"

"No, no," he interrupted. "We are discussing in Netherlands. The support group for St. Anthony's Hospital." He smiled broadly. "I am a tropical doctor and served in St. Anthony's Hospital in 1969, you see. We know the hospital needs a strong support, and the committee is *en*thusiastic to build it back up." He let the *en* do the work, like a locomotive, with the other four syllables pulled along.

"Oh." She wasn't sure where to begin, or even whether to. "OK, but I'm on my way to make rounds now on the male ward—Mondays are usually pretty busy. Would you like to join me? Perhaps it would give you a picture of how things are here. Then maybe we could talk some around ten or eleven?"

"It is unnecessary to get this picture. I know very well the sitooation here." He smiled broadly again. "All members of the committee agreed that we should talk first."

Linda turned to the assistant matron. "Well, it looks like Dr. van der Stoeckle needs to talk now. Are there any urgent patients that need to be seen on the male ward?"

The matron found her escape. "Until I confirm. I will come back to you. You are most welcome to use my office."

Dr. van der Stoeckle swept his left arm in a gracious "you first" gesture, and followed Linda into the office. The assistant matron's desk divided the small room; behind it were her chair and a potted vine on the windowsill; in front, two armless wooden chairs faced each other.

They sat, and Linda said, "Well, how can we help you?"

The broad grin again. "Well, the real question is, how can we help *you*?" He gave a staccato, cartoon-like "Ha ha!"

"I guess, Dr. van der Stoeckle, you'll—"

"Please. We are both professionals. Call me Hans."

"Fine. Well, *Hans*, maybe if you just tell me why the committee agreed that you should talk with me first."

"Yes. Yes, of course." And Hans proceeded to spin out a plan to reopen St. Anthony's as a full hospital, staffed by short-term retired Dutch tropical doctors.

Linda tried not to look annoyed as he told her the history of the mission hospital where she had spent over ten years, and this grandiose plan to reopen it. That plan somehow involved European Union money to fund a massive public health program—the "NMPSP"—which involved going house to house to screen all Kenyans for twenty diseases.

"Oh gosh. St. Anthony's was such a nice place to work," Linda admitted. "Here at the District Hospital we struggle. There aren't enough drugs or nurses; morale is poor."

Hans opened his mouth to speak, and Linda, ready to defer, paused a moment. "But—" she started just as he began: "Patients are here. Patients who need care are here—" and she suddenly stopped. Hans waited.

"Listen, Hans, I need to make rounds. We need to talk some more. How long are you around for?"

"I am on the twenty-two thirty-seven KLM flight to Amsterdam Saturday night out of Nairobi."

"OK. Can we talk again Wednesday or Thursday afternoon?"

"On my side, I am finished. I come back Wednesday and collect your answer to bring to the support group."

"OK. Come around three thirty and we'll, um… we'll talk some more."

*

With Dr. van der Stoeckle dispatched, Linda began her hospital rounds in the open ward, which was divided into cubicles of eight beds each. Her work was so automatic she no longer noticed the smell of urine and chatter of the ward TV. But today, by the third patient, she had to break stride. The bed had two patients lying head to foot. The one she saw first was a man lying on his back, ashen and clammy. She took his pulse: his wrist was cold, his pulse rapid and weak. She asked how he felt, and he groaned. She called the nurse to join her.

"Salome, do you know what the story is with this fellow?"

"Yes, Daktari. He came in with abdominal pain, yesterday but one. The clinical officer ordered fluids and surgical review. We called Dr. Kasamani and he said to prepare him for theater the next morning, that is yesterday. Anesthesia reviewed the patient yesterday and said he was not in a good condition to take to theater, and to give more fluids."

"Well, yes, he sure is dry. Where is the IV?"

"Infiltrated."

"Oh. Well, what did Dr. Kasamani say?"

"By the time I left yesterday he had not come yet. He should be coming now."

"OK. Could you please restart the IV? And hang

a bottle of normal saline, wide open." She turned to the patient. *"Habari Mzee. Unasikia uchungu?"* The man nodded and pointed to his belly. Linda slid the man's shirt up and untied the knot in his frayed rope belt. She lightly tapped on his belly: it sounded like a drum. She pressed a bit, and he winced. She removed her hand quickly and his face contorted. She flipped through the patient's file; it was almost empty. "Um, Salome, was there a hemogram done?"

"The lab says they are out of reagents."

"An abdominal film?"

"The radiographer is on the way coming."

Linda walked out into the corridor and dialed on her cell phone. "Good morning, Dr. Kasamani… Did they notify you about this fellow with the acute abdomen?… Yes, well he is still dry now, but I think by midday he should be ready… I'll call them. What time should I say you'll start?… Well, I can certainly get more history, but I'd be more comfortable if you… OK, but I really would prefer… Sure. OK." She slipped her phone back in her pocket. "Salome, could you ask the anesthetist to come back this morning? I want to cut no later than two. And please, if Kasamani comes, have him come to theater first."

By one p.m. she had seen another thirty or so male patients, interrupted by the call to pediatrics where an infant was collapsing—in fact dead. A nurse was trying to resuscitate the baby with an adult-size Ambu mask, and had called Linda because the ward doctor, Dr. Ng'etich, was just finishing a C-section. She went back to the men with pneumonias or strokes or catheters awaiting surgery for their big prostates, skipped the cubicle with men in traction, and tried to sort out the skinny coughing men in the last cubicle, appropriately called "Isolation" because it isolated those who didn't look or smell good.

By one thirty the first bottle of IV fluids for the patient who needed surgery was still a quarter full. She looked for a nurse and found only Salome trying to handle three new admissions at the nurse's station. "Um, Salome, do you know where the other nurses are?"

"I am alone, Daktari."

Linda went back to the patient with another bottle of normal saline and changed bottles as soon as the first had run in. She came back at two, called the anesthetist, and by three was scrubbing.

The belly was full of pus. She asked the nurse to turn on the suction machine, which rattled and bounced as she put the suction catheter into the belly and sucked out the pus. Then she started examining the gut. There were several perforations, and then a section that looked dusky. She started to repair each perforation, and noticed the anesthetist starting another IV. "Blood pressure?" she asked.

"Ninety systolic," he mumbled.

"Could someone please see if Kasamani has come?" she said, head bent over the incision.

Twenty minutes later, Dr. Kasamani poked his head into the theater. Linda looked up. "Daktari, could you scrub in, please?"

In a short time he was standing opposite her, gowned and gloved. "Well, what have we got here? Oh yes. Intestinal clamps, please." And before she had a chance to explain what she was doing and why, he had resected a large section of gut and was starting the anastomosis. In no time, it seemed to her, he was done—and the blood pressure had started to come up.

"Well, thank you, Daktari."

He was removing his gloves and smiled: that smile that filled his whole round face. "Not at all. Make sure he's on ceftriaxone and steroids," he said, and was gone before she could tell him that there was no ceftriaxone in the hospital pharmacy.

*

The next day her patient was still alive and now in a bed by himself. "Has Kasamani come by yet?" she asked Salome.

"No. It's Tuesday." That, apparently, was the explanation.

"OK, can we get started on rounds?"

"I am alone again, Daktari. I am right here if you need me."

Wednesday morning she found another man in her patient's bed, an old man groaning, surrounded by several relatives. Before she got the details of her patient's death, the assistant matron walked up to her with Dr. Hans van der Stoeckle right behind. "Ah, Linda," he began, "I see you have a man who is having some pain."

"Yes."

"You are using what these days to treat pains?"

"It depends on the cause. Of course, if the man has—"

"No, I am referencing *any* kind of pain. We used to remark in St. Anthony's how stoic these people are. But I'm sure you know the latest research. There is strong evidence that pain itself inhibits healing. We are very clear on this in the Netherlands."

"Yes, for sure. Here the, um, the situation, um… Well. That's a topic we'll need to discuss, maybe another time. But I guess you've come to talk some more about St. Anthony's."

"Of course."

"Let's find a corner here and sit."

The "corner" they found was a bench like a church pew in front of a waist-high wall separating two cubicles. Hans turned toward Linda, and this time just waited—and smiled.

Linda took a breath. A mentally disturbed patient reached down to touch van der Stoeckle's bushy eyebrows, but his caretaker grabbed his hand and led him away. A Nigerian soap opera blared from the ward TV. A dropped metal urinal clattered on the floor. "So, you'd like to upgrade St. Anthony's to a hospital again?" Linda began.

Hans's response was the same broad smile.

"What exactly do you mean by an upgrade?" Linda continued. "What sorts of things are donors willing to pay for?"

"Yes, yes. The equipments there need replacing, we need an ultrasound machine, and the donors are able to computerize the finance office. Then, in some months after those systems are working, electronic medical records. Oh yes, it will be a very modern hospital."

"OK, equipment is important. But the reason I came here was because the number of patients we had there was getting less every month. They just weren't coming because they couldn't afford us. Would there be a way to subsidize their hospital fees?"

"Not sustainable," said Hans. "But when we offer a quality modern service, we will draw the patients. Even from other towns we will draw them. People want good care, and we provide good care. We attract good Kenyan doctors, we build their capacity with our Dutch volunteers, and we improve the health of the community. And you are here twenty years: you are almost Kenyan. You can be the first Kenyan doctor! Ha ha!"

"Well, one thing is sure: I am *not* almost Kenyan." She paused and sighed. "The last two days were bad, and it would be *so* nice to work again at a place where there are enough medicines and nurses, where people don't die from neglect… But I know *these* people couldn't afford St. Anthony's. Isn't there any way the donors could offer subsidized care?"

Hans scowled. "The support group must be consulted. There is so much dependency, and subsidy is not sustainable. The donors want to be finished in five years. But there are so many Dutch volunteers. We come two weeks, four weeks, up to two months. We are ready." The scowl faded.

"Oh boy. Hans, I tell you what. I need to think about this. Please ask the support group if there's any way to reduce the fees so the people who need the care can afford it. I don't know how long I can stay here. But I can't go back to St. Anthony's if the patients who need care aren't there. Do you have my email? Here, write me when you find out something, OK?"

Hans stood up, eyebrows twitching. He shook Linda's hand, and left. Above the clamor of the TV, a pastor prayed loudly for the old man groaning in bed.

*

That evening, Linda wondered when van der Stoeckle would write back and whether he would really take seriously some sort of subsidy for patients. As she wondered whether she might be able to return to St. Anthony's, her phone rang. It was Walter Jorgensen, a missionary doctor who kept coming back for short stints. She had occasionally seen him at medical meetings—someone who loved to talk, she remembered. She sat down with the cat on her lap and listened.

He talked for the twenty minutes with her saying only "mm-hmm," "yes," and "OK," and then the conversation was over, and she tried to figure out what Walt wanted. He kept talking about some big screening program by its initials, and Linda finally realized it was the same thing van der Stoeckle had mentioned in passing. It must be a pretty big initiative—and there must be a lot of money involved. But what did it have to do with St. Anthony's? She tried to tease out from all of Walt's words what he wanted from her. It seemed to come down to this: the nationwide screening program would be carried out by district and mission hospitals, and he seemed to think that each facility would be given a large area to screen—and the money to do it. That money, of course, would bring in new staff and equipment, which could also be used for patient care. With some of these running costs covered, he felt, the savings could be used to lower patient fees—and St. Anthony's could become a hospital again. His concern was that as St. Anthony's was so close to the District Hospital, it wasn't likely that both would be chosen for the screening program. He saw this as a chance to be proactive and seek the contract, bringing attention—and money—to a mission hospital.

The cat whined at the door, and she absentmindedly let her out. So, she had finally gotten to ask when he slowed down, what does all that have to do with me? I work at the District. But to Walt she was still a missionary doctor, and that meant she probably wanted to return to St. Anthony's. Therefore, he assumed, she would want to pursue the screening program and all its money so she could return.

She did not tell him that he had just touched a tender spot. She did not share her frustrations about the District, or the visit from van der Stoeckle. She did not say that if St. Anthony's was upgraded to a hospital and the patients were going there, she'd go back tomorrow. She did not even know if she would.

The cat sat outside the door crying.


# 2


LEONARD MLONGO, MBChB, MMed Obs and Gyn, FRCOG, had been director of the AIDS Institute for the last six months. His office was at the front corner on the second floor of a five-story building downtown that the Institute had leased. If he had worked for the Ministry of Health for fifteen years, he'd have had no office. If he was with the School of Medicine, he'd have started out sharing an office, and would have had his own after five years. He had been with the AIDS Institute for just two years, and he'd started with his own office and a secretary. As director, he occupied an office suite and had an office staff of seven who reported directly to him. His secretary was particularly good: on his desk was a note from her that Dr. Hellen Nyalo from the School of Medicine had rung asking for a few minutes with him this morning.

One reason Mlongo did well with Western NGOs— the founders and funders of the AIDS Institute—was that he was personable, polished, and efficient. And he looked the part: tall, handsome, with a strong, resonant voice. And since Western donors had for decades been funding anything to do with women, children, and sex, his decision to become a reproductive-health specialist had been excellent.

On his desk was a tiny bas-relief sculpture of a woman, her partner, and two children, one child obviously older than the other. He picked it up and turned it in his hands. The figures were made from refashioned intrauterine devices: several types of wire and plastic IUDs bent to form the members of a planned family.

The plastic-encased sculpture had been presented to him by an NGO that, several years previously, had hired him to train Ministry of Health doctors in the technique of inserting IUDs in women as soon as they delivered, while they were still on the delivery couch.

"So, how many children did your mother have?" his American supervisor from the IUD job had asked him as they were driving to a remote district hospital to demonstrate IUD insertion.

"I was one of seven," Mlongo had answered. "Nine, actually, but two died."

"And you?" she pushed. "How many do you want?"

He grinned. "Two," he answered quickly; then, after a brief pause, "of course."

She laughed. "But your wife…by the way, are you married?"

"We are on the way."

"So how many children do you think your wife wants?"

"She will agree to two."

"She *will* agree?" the supervisor laughed again. "Are you suggesting that she doesn't agree yet?"

"Oh, no. She agrees. My wife is a teacher, you see, and she sometimes loses half her class each year because the families have no school fees. She knows the problems with having too many children. Look there." He pointed out the window as they slowed down, going through a small village. "What are those children do-ing playing now? Why aren't they in school?"

The scene, which the supervisor saw on every village trip, suddenly seemed less cheerful. "I never thought of that—but of course. At nine in the morning, why aren't they in school?"

"Yes, there are simply too many children…"

"And that's exactly why we are here!" she burst out.

Mlongo continued: "…who don't have school fees." He paused. "So, yes, in our work we are certainly on the right path. Do you say the right path or the right road?"

"Oh, either one, I guess. I say the right track."

*

The IUD sculpture on Mlongo's desk was overshad-owed by a much larger sculpture of the red AIDS ribbon, formed from red ARV pills fastened together like Legos. He was just replacing the IUD sculpture next to the red ribbon when there was a brief knock on the door. It cracked open, and Hellen poked her head in. "Mlongo? Are you busy?"

Mlongo stood. He was wearing a bright orange-and-blue embroidered dashiki. "Hellen, come right in! No, my board meeting doesn't start till ten, and my secretary told me you were coming."

Dr. Hellen Nyalo, senior lecturer in epidemiology, walked in and quietly closed the door. Her hair was plaited with long extensions, and she wore a red blouse with a white scarf and grey slacks. Her age was hidden between her trim figure and her canny face.

"Sit down, Hellen! Now, let me guess: you've got some students who want to do a project on discordant couples."

Hellen chuckled and sat on one of the upholstered wooden armchairs in front of Mlongo's massive desk. "No, I—"

"OK, you need some Fluconazole for a toenail-fungus campaign."

"No, no, I just—"

"You just want to borrow a couple reams of paper?"

"Mlongo!" She was laughing. "Do I always come here begging?"

"No, not *always*. Just most of the time—at least when I worked downstairs. So, now that I'm in this office?"

"No, no, no. Actually, I come with some news—but maybe you already know. I was in Washington the other week, getting updates on the National Multi-Phasic Screening Program…"

"Oh, yes. We'll likely be coordinating the implementation here. And you?"

"Well, I think we're in a pretty good position to do the evaluation piece."

Mlongo reflected a minute, then said, "You know

we have a research department now—in fact, we'll be getting our third PhD researcher from the States next month. I wonder if this evaluation piece is something I should approach our board about pursuing."

"Sure, you could do that. But the Medical Research Council are the ones who now have to approve all big research projects. It's a pretty rigorous process."

"Unless you know someone."

"Well, yes."

"Which you do?"

Hellen flicked her eyebrows up.

"I see," said Mlongo. "So you are thinking it might be smoother if the Institute moves ahead with the screening campaign, and the School of Medicine concentrates on research."

"Of course, if your board wants to try to navigate the Research Council…"

Mlongo smiled. "I think they'll be pretty busy just focusing on the screening campaign itself. Now, if you need to contract a PhD biostatistician, you know where to find one."

"That's already in my plans. Thanks, Mlongo."

*

That afternoon, Mlongo had a visit from Gillian Peel, a tall, striking British doctor of thirty-seven. She wore her brown hair shoulder length and her tops low cut. She had spent most of her time since qualifying working in

East Africa for relief agencies. Her first was Médecins Sans Frontières, and she returned with them often, to Somalia, Congo, Sudan, Burundi. She came to Kenya for R & R, and once for relief work, during the Mount Elgon trouble. It was there she met Mlongo, when he also was doing a stint with MSF before joining the AIDS Institute.

"Gillian!" Mlongo stood as she came in. "What brings you to a place where there is no war, famine, or earthquake?"

"Hey, Len," she said, as if she'd just seen him yesterday. "How come you're still working in a place with no war, famine, or earthquake?" Her smile seemed like an afterthought.

"Well, Gillian—please, sit down—we *are* in a war here. The war against AIDS. And you've probably heard, we have one of the best armies in Kenya. We have already enrolled—"

"Bollocks!" She cut him off, still wearing that enticing smile. And still standing. "You don't have to give me that PR. I know you're good. And of course AIDS work is important. But come on, Len, everyone's doing AIDS work now. Doesn't it get sort of, you know, boring?"

"For someone who gets energized by shrapnel wounds, I suppose AIDS work is, as you put it, boring."

"Bloody hell, you know I'm not a surgeon, and most of the time we're just trying to provide basic health care for civilians chased out of their villages. But *all* of their care, not just AIDS care. I mean it's just wrong when those kids die because their parents have been chased off their farms and can't feed them. Or when those mums die from obstructed labor because it's not safe for them to travel to the hospital. Or when those women get raped by the soldiers and get AIDS. Does all that energize me? That's not the point. It's just work that needs to be done."

Mlongo paused a moment before responding. "Yes, Gillian, that is very important work."

"Right." She finally sat. "Hey, nice chair! So how've you been?"

"Well, you can see I'm doing quite well." He ran a finger along his desk. "And you? What brings you here? More R & R?"

"Yes, but I'm also sort of in between jobs. Some stuff has come up back home, and I need to be more, um…available."

"So you're going back to UK?"

"Not if I can help it. I think I just want to look around here a bit."

"You mean *here* here? Or here Kenya?"

"Probably here Kenya. You're pretty well connected. I wondered if you knew of anything…well, anything available for a few months that might be a little less, mmm, remote."

"And not connected with AIDS."

"OK, I'm not looking for AIDS work—but I wouldn't turn it down either."

"Interesting you should come in now. I was just talking with a researcher from the School of Medicine." And Mlongo laid out to her the idea of the NMPSP, and the likelihood that the AIDS Institute was well positioned to be involved.

"All very interesting. But I can't see how any of that could involve me."

"Well, we have experience with the home counseling and testing program we've been doing for HIV. So now we can expand our screening beyond AIDS."

"OK…" She cocked her head.

"But also beyond our catchment area. We have the capacity to do a lot of the screening in northern Kenya, where all those refugees are, and where no one else is set up to do that."

"You mean Kakuma? Dadaab? But that's the other side of the country!"

"We live in Kenya, my dear. We are *linked*." He held up his cell phone. "We could easily set up satellite offices. And you are just the person to get us started."

Gillian sat back a moment and said, as much to herself as to Mlongo, "Screening. Screening? *Screening?* You're going to screen these refugees and nomads for hypertension and diabetes? People that we already know need basic health care? Does that really make sense?"

"That's an excellent question, Gillian—and I think comes to the core of how the Institute could make this program really work for Kenyans. First, we have developed a lot of expertise in finding and treating one chronic disease, AIDS. Now it's time to apply that to all the other chronic diseases Kenyans have that are being ignored. But more than this, you are right about refugees and pastoralists needing basic health care. This program will be screening not just for chronic diseases, but for so many risk factors as well. Now, here's the key: there are lots of NGOs working in those refugee camps. A program like this will give them immense amounts of data, and get patients to them at a much earlier stage in their illness—even if it's TB or malnutrition. The point is, this program can answer exactly the question you asked on whether this makes sense—*if* the Institute gets the contract. And if *you* agree to set up the program." He gave a slight smile.

"Brilliant," she said, expressionless.

"I can never tell with you, Gillian, what you mean by *brilliant*. Do you mean it is a brilliant program? Do you mean you'll do it? Or are you doing one of those sarcastic things that we don't get?"

"No, Lenny, it's honestly brilliant. You're brilliant. Let me check a few things and I'll get back with you. Cheers!" And she was gone.

# Surveillance Medicine

## 1

ABOUT TWO MONTHS after the call from Walt, Linda received an email from Hans van der Stoeckle, informing her that he would be returning to St. Anthony's for an extended visit of one month. He was coming with his wife who, he said, was a retired communication specialist, and together they would be doing some workshops for the nurses at St. Anthony's on "How to Break Bad News." Hans was inviting Linda and "your staff at the district" to take advantage of these workshops. And, he added, since the Dutch support group for St. Anthony's had arranged for the patient subsidy—surely she had already heard—did he assume correctly that she was returning to St. Anthony's?

The previous two months had been particularly bad. Linda had not seen Kasamani at all over the last five weeks, and in that time one of her patients had died on the operating table. The woman had arrived one morning with a full-term pregnancy saying she had pain in her belly, and that her labor, which was strong the night before, had stopped. Linda noted immediately that the woman was pale and looked scared. For good reason. With a quick, gentle exam, Linda felt several unusual bumps in the abdomen: the baby lying outside the uterus, just under the skin and thin abdominal wall. She assumed the woman had ruptured her uterus during the night—she would get the details later—and told the nurse to call the anesthetist while she scrubbed.

Ten minutes later, Dr. Ng'etich arrived and immediately began adjusting the IVs and giving medications.

"Hello Ng'etich. Are you scrubbing in?"

"Sorry, Linda, I cannot. I will administer the ketamine."

"Ketamine? Why ketamine?"

"The anesthetist cannot be found. I cannot give the usual anesthesia, but at least you can do the needful for the patient under ketamine."

While she was putting on her gloves and gown, one of the nurses filled in a bit more history: the night before, the woman had gone to a traditional birth attendant, who noticed the baby's arm sticking out. She tried to push the arm back in, while the husband went looking for a vehicle. He was unable to find any until the *matatus* started running in the morning. The baby never came out—and then the pain increased and the labor stopped.

Linda scrubbed the belly, draped the woman, and looked toward Ng'etich, who nodded. She incised. As soon as she got through the abdominal wall, she saw a small leg and arm, and a belly full of blood. She removed the dead fetus, handed it to the nurse, and suctioned out the blood. The uterus was ripped on one side, and the edges were bleeding. She started rapidly clamping the edges that were oozing, found the uterine artery and clamped it, and then began putting clamps on the rest of the uterus that was still attached, so she could remove it. Her technique was effective but not polished: there was no longer any bleeding and the patient was still breathing, but the operative site was full of clamps. Now she had to go one by one, tying off the bleeders as she removed each clamp.

She had tied off two when she noticed Ng'etich in motion: changing an IV, palpating for pulses, listening to the chest, and then trying to intubate the patient. She paused. He began external chest compressions. She stood back, breathed deeply, and arched her neck backward. They had lost the patient.

But those deaths on the operating table were only the most dramatic disasters, the exposed eyes and ears of the submerged hippopotamus. Underneath, at the rate of almost one a day, were the children who died. Linda had gotten used to it—sort of, as long as she didn't come home and think too deeply. But when she got van der Stoeckle's email about the support coming for St. Anthony's, she *did* think of the children who had died in the last few days.

Some had simply come too late. It was the other half of the deaths that made Linda keep looking back to van der Stoeckle's email. Last Saturday, the clinical officer had admitted a three-year-old girl with "cerebral malaria"—fever and convulsions. The orders were simple: malaria test and quinine IV. No one summoned the doctor on call. By Sunday, the malaria test was back—negative. Monday morning, Ng'etich had seen the little girl, who was markedly worse. He touched her: she was hot. He tried to bend her neck: it was stiff. He did a lumbar puncture, which showed pus in the spinal fluid. The girl had meningitis that had been missed. He started the antibiotics—and though the fever came down, the girl never woke up.

The next day Linda was on pediatrics because Ng'etich asked her to cover for him: he had not received his salary for the last two months and had to travel to Nairobi to sort it out. He didn't seem worried. He said it happened almost every year, and after a week of daily appearances at the Ministry of Health, he was sure it would be reinstated.

In the second cubicle, Linda saw a skinny, dehydrated baby with a high-pitched cry. She assumed the baby had just been brought in and asked the nurse to bring a new file, start an IV, and begin hydration. Then she noticed an IV line in the baby's hand, but no IV fluids running. The nurse brought the file, which had already been started. The child had arrived at the hospital thirty-six hours previously, hadn't gotten to the ward until after Ng'etich had left yesterday, and had been given absolutely no treatment, except the placing of the IV line, which hadn't been used.

Linda spoke sharply: "Bring a bottle of normal saline. Quickly! Why hasn't this child had any fluids yet?"

The nurse fumbled. "I have just now reported, Daktari. Unless I confirm with the nurse from the night shift."

"Well, don't do that now. Just get the fluids going." Linda looked around. "By the way, where are the other nurses?"

"It is just me until my colleague joins me on split shift this afternoon."

"And how many children are on the ward now?" Linda's tone was already softening.

"Sixty-four."

As Linda and the nurse were setting up the IV fluids, Linda murmured, half to herself, "Why don't we have more nurses?"

"We are asking the same, Daktari," the nurse said. "There are plenty of nurses in Kenya, but they don't hire them. Imagine!"

"But why don't they hire enough nurses?"

"I don't know. I heard it was because of the World Bank."

"The World Bank? They won't let the Ministry hire nurses?"

"That's what I heard—World Bank or IMF, I'm

not sure. You know, structural adjustment. They said nurses don't make money for the economy, I guess."

Sometimes Linda had to watch the children die; sometimes she just found an empty bed in the morning, or watched a small bundle being wheeled to the mortuary on a trolley. Or she'd remember only at the end of the week that a seven-year-old girl with burns over a third of her body was admitted on Tuesday, but she hadn't seen her after that.

*

Two days later, Walt called as Linda was leaving the hospital. She listened to him as she walked home, past the couch and coffin makers. He was back in Kenya, he said, and wanted to fill her in about developments around the NMPSP. She undoubtedly had heard that it was up and running, and that mission hospitals were poised to play a significant role.

She hadn't heard.

"So," Walt continued, "this might be *the* God-given opportunity to get mission hospitals back in the picture, big time. Remember Esther and 'for such a time as this'?"

"Uh…no."

"Well, anyway, here's what I'd like to do. Let's convene reps from all the mission hospitals and see if we can come together with some sort of unified voice about how ideally placed we are to do this screening. We can show that we've moved from free hospitals for remote poor people to first-rate modern institutions, deeply committed to public health."

By this time she was passing the place where the two young men had been making bricks. Now completely dried, they were being stacked for firing. The bricks themselves were the kiln: stacked to make an opening for the firebox at the bottom, the whole pile covered with dried mud; stacked just high enough so they would all be well fired. She barely listened as Walt droned on about screening. He asked if she would come to this gathering of mission hospitals.

She had been working for ten years in the same hospital and nothing was getting better. Hearing that St. Anthony's was reopening enabled her to realize how weary she was. What would she lose by going to the mission hospital meeting? Perhaps just to get Walt off her back, she told him she would come.

## 2

The next morning, when Linda arrived back at the hospital, Dr. Hans van der Stoeckle was waiting for her in the matron's office, already wearing a broad smile. "I have returned," he proclaimed, "together with my wife, Mieke. We have begun the lectures on Breaking

Bad News, and the nurses at St. Anthony's are very *en*thusiastic. Up to now they have never been taught this, and they ask my wife to stay and give lectures every day! Ha! Ha ha!"

"Welcome back, Hans. I'm glad the classes are going well."

"Yes, but these are just a small beginning. Has the diocese invited you back to St. Anthony's?"

"No, I haven't heard anything from them."

"You will. You very much will. They did not tell you they have decided to reopen St. Anthony's as a *hospital?* They rely for now on the Dutch support. And you."

"And *me?* Funny they haven't said anything…"

"I was with them yesterday, and they begin already to prepare the letter of invitation to you."

"OK, but what about the subsidy for patients who can't afford the care there?"

"Yes, yes, of course! I wrote you already that this problem is solved. The support group in the Netherlands has developed a patient-subsidy program, which my wife, Mieke, is organizing. She will give you details."

Now van der Stoeckle had the answer to Kenya's problems, just as Walt had the night before. She mumbled an excuse about needing to see a patient, and promised to get back to him tomorrow.

She *did* need to see a patient—a five-year-old boy who had pneumonia and wasn't getting better. She went directly to his bedside and found him sitting propped up, looking terrible, his breathing shallow and rapid, nostrils flaring with each inhalation. She examined him quickly: he was hot, and the findings in his chest were worse than when she'd left him yesterday. She looked at the file: all the antibiotics she'd ordered had a tick next to them, and then a little scribble next to the tick. She looked more closely: "o/s"—out of stock. Ticked, but not given because there were none to give.

She asked the boy's father, who was sitting beside the bed, how he was doing. He explained that the nurses told him to go to the local pharmacy and buy the necessary antibiotic because the hospital had run out. But, he said, he had no money. So, how many days since the boy had had his medication? Five. Linda jammed her hand into her pocket and tugged out a wad of cash. She shoved a thousand-shilling note into the man's hand. "Thank you, Daktari." Thank you because you have paid for one day of this expensive antibiotic which the boy now needs—needs because he was given off-and-on doses of the normal antibiotic until his infection developed resistance to it. Thank you for ensuring that children get one more day of the free hospital care they have been promised by the government. Thank you, in other words, for subsidizing rich, corrupt Nairobi politicians.

Linda was aware of her slow fuse, the one most people never knew was lit. Bill had known, of course.

Bill had often seen the fuse smolder, only to be doused before the explosion. He had even seen the explosion once or twice. But Bill had died of cancer ten years ago, and the fuse burned slowly enough that Linda found herself pretending it wasn't lit. Now she could not deny it: it was lit, and she began to worry what sort of explosion would happen. And so she surprised even herself when she finished the note on the five-year-old boy and, while walking home, called Hans on her cell phone and told him that she was moving back to St. Anthony's.

Since St. Anthony's had become a possibility, she had been thinking more about the patients she treated every day at the District that she could do nothing for—patients she could not otherwise permit herself to dwell on. And now, aware again of her slow fuse, she thought of Bill, whom she hadn't really thought about for months.

Of course, she never stopped being aware of his absence: his picture was on her bureau, along with pictures of their two children. Two of his shirts were still in her closet, shirts she used as jackets. She had long ago stopped mourning his death—unless, of course, she looked at some of the pictures in the albums, or listened to his voice on the few tapes she still kept, or read over some of his handwritten notes. If she stumbled across the pictures or notes while looking for something else, and sat down and looked and read and remembered, then she would cry again. Alone, quietly. And then carefully replace the pictures and notes and tapes, and get back to what she was doing.

But, she was realizing now, those were times when she mourned *her* loss, not Bill's. She had lost Bill, but *he*, of course, had lost his life. Bill, the one who knew about her fuse, the one she could safely yell at because he loved her. Bill, who had lost his life nearly ten years ago, but whose loss had started ten years before that— a loss she suspected but he always denied. He said he *enjoyed* staying at home, watching Josh and Angie grow. And as they went to school, he said he *preferred* to be home, where he could write.

But didn't he miss the classroom at the university, where he engaged (so well, she knew) with his students? Where, on the occasions when he could sidestep the dross of university politics, he came home electrified by ideas in his field of agriculture economics? And then there was his research proposal, the one to test his ideas with Kenyan farmers; the one that never got funded. Yes, he would admit, he did enjoy the academic life— but now Kenya was home, and these also were good times.

They *were* good times, those years at St. Anthony's. And for those ten years her best friend would listen to her and reflect on what she said, and she in turn would engage with him about his ideas and writings…and somewhere deep beneath the words she knew that he had lost a formal academic life so she could have her life at St. Anthony's.

They were still at St. Anthony's when Bill died, though she and Bill had talked a lot about the declining number of patients and what her options were. And when St. Anthony's downgraded to a health center within a year after Bill's death it seemed a good time to move. It had been lonely there without Bill, and with their kids now on their own, she knew she needed to start again somewhere else. Moving to the District had been exactly the right thing at the time.

The fuse had been smoldering again, only she was without her best friend, the one who understood her fuse; she was on her own, having her arguments with herself. And she had just made a decision that extinguished her fuse.

She walked home, past the big empty billboard, around the honking *matatus*, around the corner where a dozen motorcycle taxis waited for passengers; off the main road, where children left their ball of bound plastic bags to run up and shake her hand; past the brick kiln, which was now being dismantled, the red-orange bricks neatly stacked; on down toward the big trees outside her compound. By the time she came into her compound she was smiling, and tears were pouring down her face.

Mercy—middle-aged, stout, wearing a functional housedress—had just finished and was walking out the door when Linda entered the compound. Mercy looked at her face, and without saying a word swallowed her in a long, tight hug. After a minute she pulled back and gave a little twitch of the head to ask what the tears were for. Linda said only, "Bill," and Mercy nodded, her own eyes wet, and hugged Linda again. Then Mercy said, "Linda, come with me to mass early tomorrow morning."

Linda swallowed and wiped her cheeks with a sleeve. "I would like that. Thank you."

*

The daily mass was small, brief, intimate. Less than twenty people were there, half of them nuns who taught at the schools. After the confession they sang:

*Utuhurumie, eh Bwana, eh Bwana, eh Bwana,*
*Tuhurumie, eh Bwana, eh Bwana, eh Bwana,*
*Bwana utuhurumie*

Sometimes Linda just entered the music, or let it enter her. On Sunday morning, with the large choir leading, the music often flowed through her, but this morning, with just a few reedy voices singing, she found herself translating: "Lord, have mercy." She had wanted the mass to carry her, but now she started carrying it—or at least the part her mind had just grabbed. And as she carried that part, the mass went on, but she didn't.

Lord, have mercy. Oh God. Lord have mercy on that boy with pneumonia—if he's still alive—the boy who wasn't getting his medicines. Lord have mercy on that frustrating, pathetic hospital that can't even provide the medicines and nurses to treat the boy. Lord have mercy on this sad country that so often gets derailed providing for its own. Lord have mercy on all those patients who can't afford St. Anthony's. She paused in her litany. And Lord have mercy on all those who, by what they have done and what they have failed to do, have caused this…this…mess.

They were already in the readings, but Linda couldn't get past mercy. And Lord, have mercy on me. I just…don't…get it.

3

She *didn't* get it—but what she did get was rising the next morning, every next morning, and going to work. So ten days later, when Walt called to remind her about the workshop, it was an intrusion into her every-morning schedule, taking her away from little Nafuna with her painful sickle cell disease and grouchy old Ndege with his out-of-control blood pressure. But she had made a commitment, and she would keep it. Two days later she flew to Nairobi for Walt's workshop.

The Protestant Health Council Retreat Center had that distinctive Kenyan ostentatious humility: gold-painted pillars in front of the main meeting hall, stacked plastic funeral chairs inside, and two toilets out of order in the ladies' room. Walt strode into the meeting hall ten minutes late, sweating, carrying a pile of loosely collated documents. The top set slipped onto the floor as he was laying them on the table, and three participants in the front row jumped up to gather the papers.

Walt looked around the room. "Does anyone have those, you know, office pins? You know, the kind you use when you attach a piece of carbon paper to a document you want to make a copy of?" Blank looks. "Couldn't find the stapler—well, I found the stapler, but I couldn't find staples."

He talked continuously as he rearranged his papers, then addressed the fifteen or so participants in the workshop—about half missionaries from the larger mission hospitals, the other half Kenyans. He had prepared a PowerPoint presentation to introduce the National Multi-Phasic Screening Program. Once they'd gone through that, he divided the participants—doctors, nurses, administrators—into groups, each with a newsprint flipchart and markers to record their discussions. At the end he had them present their group work in plenary, then helped the group develop a resolution as a press release. This step went rapidly, because it was the end of the day, and also because Walt had prepared a rough draft beforehand. The participants ended up resolving that the church hospitals of the Protestant Health Council (hereinafter "The Council") supported the concept of the National Multi-Phasic Screening Program (hereinafter "NMPSP") and declared their availability as "private" participants in the public–private partnerships, and so on.

After the meeting, Walt put on his logistics hat, ensuring everyone had transport home. When that was over, he called a cab and accompanied Linda to the airport. He had wanted to pick her brain, he told her, and what better place than being "captive" together—his fingers made the quotes—in a cab. As the cab driver shoehorned them into the bumper-to-bumper traffic on Waiyaki Way, Walt asked Linda if St. Anthony's would be involved in the NMPSP.

"There's a lot to think about here," said Linda, "but I can't speak for St. Anthony's. I haven't really started working back there yet. This will take a lot of thought and discussion."

"OK, sure: you need to think and discuss. But I'm really interested in what *you* think. You've been around a lot longer than I have. Do you think you can get St. Anthony's involved?"

Linda sat thinking, and Walt assumed her silence was an answer.

"OK," he said. "Do you *want* to help St. Anthony's get involved in screening? Do you buy all this? Talk to me."

"You know, Walt," Linda began, aware that another slow fuse had been lit, "I'd like to answer you, but it's awfully hard while you're talking." She glanced at him, but Walt said nothing. "So I'll tell you what I've been thinking. First, I'm a doctor. Not a visionary, not an organizer. I was trained to take care of sick people, and that's what I do well. What I've seen over the last twenty years is that there are far too many sick people at the District and at St. Anthony's—people who need care and who all too often don't get that care. They don't get it for lots of reasons: they can't afford it, or there aren't enough nurses, or there are no medicines, or someone doesn't show up." They lurched sideways as the driver swung into a faster lane. "And it's true, I can't do much for them if we don't have nurses or medicines or IVs or sutures. But I can't just walk away, either."

She looked out the window at the gaudily painted *matatus*, now barely aware of Walt. "But I did. I just walked away from the District, because the Dutch have promised they will provide subsidies for the people who can't afford St. Anthony's. Frankly, I only half believe it; we'll see. The fact is, I'm just tired of banging my head against a wall. I need a break."

She paused again, and turned to look at Walt.

"I'm listening," he said.

"OK, now about screening. I'm sure it's a wonderful program, and I'm sure there's all sorts of evidence to support it. Frankly, I don't care. It makes no sense to go hunting for people who don't know they're sick, when we've already got so many people we can't take care of—people who know they're sick and want some help. So no, Walt, I don't buy it. I don't buy it." She tried and failed to summon a smile, and ended up just pursing her lips. "OK," she said. "Now you can talk."

Walt was sweating, so he rolled down a window; exhaust fumes billowed in. The cab slowed as they approached downtown, where all the hawkers weaved between the barely moving cars, and he rolled up the window again. He gave Linda a sidelong glance to see if she was really finished, then spoke carefully. "Those are heavy thoughts, and I know they come from your heart. There's just one more thing I'd like to get your perspective on. Now, at the meeting today there was clear affirmation of the NMPSP from the Kenyans there, didn't you think? *They* want this, so shouldn't we support what they want?"

Linda started shaking her head even before he was finished. "Oh, Walt, were we at the same meeting? This was never *their* idea. Of course they support it—you think they're going to throw away a chance for funds? We have no idea what they really think of it. Did you notice that you did most of the talking today?"

For a full minute, Walt said nothing.

Linda broke the silence. "You OK? I'm sorry. Of course you did most of the talking. You were leading the workshop."

"No, Linda, you're right. I'm just thinking that I did kind of dominate the discussion. It's just that I really believe in this thing, and…getting them to talk was, um, difficult. I mean, I really did want to know what they thought…" He trailed off. He was back at the meeting, replaying his performance. She was back at the District Hospital, astounded all over again that the screening program would do nothing for any of the patients she was picturing there.

"What will Ng'etich think of all this?" she murmured, pressing her fingers to the window. They were pulling into the airport.

"Who's Ng'etich?" Walt asked, startling her. She hadn't realized she'd spoken aloud.

"I'll tell you next time. My plane's about to board. See you, Walt. Thanks for arranging the cab."

### Somalia

**At the end of their second week, during one of their afternoon sessions sitting on the plastic chairs under the acacia, Mlongo announced, "It's Christmas today."**

**"Wow!" Linda said. "Have you been keeping track of the days?"**

"I have a calendar watch." He held it up. "I just noticed the date."

"So, how do you spend Christmas—usually, I mean?"

Mlongo was making triangles in the sand with the toe of his shoe, dragging the chain as he drew. "Oh, Monica goes to her parents' village every holiday, and takes the kids. In fact, they went there before I left for Dadaab, and planned to stay until the New Year. You have kids?"

"Yeah, but they're grown now. I think Angie was planning to spend Christmas with friends in Kinshasa—she did last year anyway. She's a journalist in Congo. And Josh—he's a grad student back in the States. He's got friends in Boston, or maybe Bill's brother had him over for the holidays."

A black-and-white daytime mosquito buzzed in Linda's ear, and she tried to squash it against her shoulder. And failed. Across the compound, two chickens pecked at a day-old cowpat.

After a while, Mlongo said, "Tell me, Linda, how did you get involved with the NMPSP?"

"Oh golly, how *did* I get involved? Well, I guess maybe I first heard from this Dutch doctor, van der Stoeckle...back, oh, maybe a year ago."

"I've never heard of that guy." For a moment Mlongo was back at the AIDS Institute, networking, wondering what part this van der Stoeckle could play at the Institute, wondering what resources he could bring. "I would have thought you'd found out from Walt. Or maybe Kasamani."

"Oh gosh. Walt. Yeah, he was part of it all, but Kasamani more so."

The conversation started to fizzle, as their conversations often did with no natural close, no "Gotta go. See you later" possible. Linda leaned her head back against the smooth trunk of the acacia and closed her eyes. But a moment later Mlongo said, as if in response to her comment, "You know, Linda, Hellen says I'm one of Us Guys." Linda looked at him, puzzled, so he explained the concept as Hellen had outlined it to him…

4

By dint of his status as honorary lecturer at the School of Medicine, Dr. Leonard Mlongo was entitled to eat at the Faculty Club. The tables were outside under white canvas awnings, and waiters dressed in black skirts or trousers, white shirts, and black bowties served food prepared in a colonial-era stone house. The club was quite busy at lunch on weekdays, leaving the waiters no time to move from table to table with the hand-washing pitcher and bowl. Instead, the guests queued at the edge of the lawn in front of a large jug with a spigot at the bottom. Mlongo and Gillian waited in line as each guest bent over to wash, legs spread wide to avoid getting splashed.

They found a small table and ordered. "Kenya's finest cuisine," Gillian said as the waiter left to get their food. "Greasy chicken or beef stew, rice or *ugali*, and greens. Nothing changes."

Mlongo laughed. "You still don't like our food? I'm rather fond of chicken and *ugali*, as long as there's plenty of greens."

She wrinkled her nose. "So listen, Len, last time we were together, a couple months ago, you said maybe I could work on your screening program. Maybe even linking MCH outreach with screening, especially in the remote areas. You were serious?"

"Of course I was serious. Why?"

"So what's involved? When can we get started?"

Mlongo started thinking out loud, meandering verbally around the administrative obstacle course necessary to create a new job. He knew how to do it, and enjoyed the challenge of linking this innovative public health effort with clinical outreach and even treatment. Just as he was getting to the roughed-out job description, the food came: the greasy chicken and *ugali* for Mlongo, the beef stew and rice for Gillian. Mlongo opened his napkin, salted his stew as he inhaled the savory steam rising from the chicken, and crafted his first ball of *ugali* with his right hand. He then bowed his head for a silent prayer. By the time he was ready to begin, Gillian had consumed nearly half of her stew.

With her fork, she turned the bone with the wad of fat attached, looking for a shred of meat. "So my responsibility would be the places densely populated with refugees, especially Kakuma and Dadaab and the surrounding areas?" she said.

He nodded, his mouth full.

"And I would be tasked to link whatever NGO out-reach activities are ongoing—and whatever little gov-ernment services are there—with the actual NMPSP surveys that the AIDS Institute will provide?"

Mlongo swallowed. "Right again."

"Now, most of the NGOs have Nairobi offices, so I'll obviously need to connect them with you here…"

"Or even with the NMPSP Nairobi office."

"OK, even better. I can do that from Nairobi, as long as I make periodic trips to those areas, paid for out of the NMPSP budget."

"That's pretty much the way I see it too. But I just remembered: you had told me earlier you had some family problems. Is everything OK?"

"Oh," she said. "Right…Well, the family is fine. It's actually just a little medical issue of my own I wanted to make sure was sorted out. You see…well, I guess if anyone would understand, you would. I had a Pap smear—three, four months ago. Before I saw you in your office, anyway. And it was pretty bad. So I had a conization done in Nairobi, and I'm supposed to get repeat smears every couple of months to make sure they got it all. That's all."

Mlongo grinned.

"You think it's funny?" she asked, trying to decide whether or not to be angry.

"Oh, no, Gillian," he said quickly. "Not funny. I'm smiling because—well, first, I'm sure it can be pretty scary to get a positive test of any kind, but you did exactly the right thing, and I'm smiling because it's already taken care of."

"So you think these other tests aren't necessary?"

"No, no, they're necessary, but I've never seen them come back positive after the procedure's been done. But I'm also smiling because you found this out through screening! What better ambassador for a screening program than someone who's been successfully screened?"

As Gillian sat back to digest Mlongo's comments, together with Kenya's finest cuisine, Dr. Hellen Nyalo walked up to them. "Mlongo, are you finally planning on joining our faculty officially?"

"No, Hellen—in fact, I was just going to ask if you were finally planning to move over to the Institute. You know we could use a researcher like you in our new—"

"Yes, new research division. You told me about that. Uh…" She looked at Gillian and offered her hand. "I'm Hellen Nyalo from the School of Medicine. You're…?"

"Goodness, Hellen, you two haven't met? Hellen, this is Dr. Gillian Peel. She and I worked together during the Mt. Elgon trouble. Now it looks like she'll be joining us in NMPSP, especially in some of the refugee camps."

"Pleasure," said Gillian.

"Good to meet you too. Uh, you two are in a meeting?"

"Oh no," said Mlongo, "we were just having lunch."

"Actually, a lunch meeting." Gillian corrected him. "But we've finished. In fact, Len has given me some assignments, and I'm off to do them. Cheers!" And she got up and left.

"Are you finishing too?" Hellen asked Mlongo.

"No, I'm here. Please join me."

Hellen ordered *dengu*, rice, and a Fanta, washed her hands, and sat down.

"So what will this Gillian person actually be doing with NMPSP?" she asked.

"Well, what Gillian and I were just talking about is how we can link the screening with existing outreach activities in some of those remote areas in and around Kakuma and Dadaab."

Hellen looked at Mlongo over her glasses. "She needs a job?"

Mlongo smiled and tipped up his chin.

When Hellen's food came, she spooned half of the rice into the *dengu* sauce, and stirred it in.

Mlongo was watching closely. "Hellen, you just put your rice *into* the *dengu*."

She looked at him quizzically, spoon suspended in midair.

"Well, most people put the sauce *over* the rice."

"Ah, yes."

"So, does it help to preserve the nutrients better or what?"

Hellen, bemused, shook her head slowly and said, "I have no idea." She ate in silence for a minute. "You do pretty well with expats," she said. "By the way."

"Oh, I've known Gillian a long time. She's got a lot of energy, and she means well."

"Kind of like Walt, uh, what's-his-name. J something?"

"You know Walt?"

"Everyone knows Walt. He's always at meetings, lectures, conferences…and he doesn't even live here."

"No, Gillian's not like that. She thinks meetings are a waste of time. She's more of one of those activist types." He paused. "But come to think of it, there are similarities. Both of them are pretty sure they know what's right."

"Yeah," Hellen said. "Walt fancies himself an expert."

"More than other *wazungu?* I guess I've got used to it."

"I guess you have." She stopped eating and looked

at him. "How do you put up with people like him and Gillian?"

He engaged her question with his eyes, but said nothing.

She went on: "OK, your pay's good, more than the university offers. But—" She looked away, and then back to the eyes. "OK, you play those games far much better than I can. Maybe it's our age difference."

"What do you mean?"

"Well, some of those old guys—like from Prof G's class—they watched their parents live under colonial rule. They learned early how to play those games. And some of them are still angry about it. With my age-mates I don't see as much anger. But you…you're what my daughter calls 'Us Guys.'"

"Us Guys?"

"Yes. She stays with her father in Nairobi, you know. Grew up there. Doesn't know her mother tongue. Almost completely detribalized. So she and her friends can't say 'us Kikuyu' or 'us Luo' or 'us Kalenjin' like their cousins upcountry. So they call themselves 'Us Guys'. But Us Guys isn't about tribe, or not mostly. It's about the life they know together, the life they see in movies and TV, the life they see on the streets downtown and in Sarit Centre, the life that's sometimes more Western than in Europe or America, but still with one foot in the village. Us Guys."

"So if I'm one of Us Guys, why aren't you?"

"OK, I grew up in Nairobi too, and I married

outside my tribe. But I think I still have some of the anger of Prof G's generation, and nowhere near the patience you guys have with the games—and with *wazungu*."

"So instead of *playing* the games, you analyze the results with your research."

Hellen washed her last bite down with Fanta. "Yeah. There's less to argue about. The numbers tell the story."

### Somalia

**Mlongo explained to Linda the idea of Us Guys, and then paused. "Now sure, people like me are somewhat detribalized—and it's true, like Hellen said, that we look for the skills that will put us in better positions economically. Why not? It's also true that we have no respect for the tribalized politics of our parents' generation." He paused again; Linda waited. "But what sticks with me—and sort of sticks me as well—is how the whole thing came up. She said I could put up with aggressive and arrogant *wazungu* better than she could. Or I was used to them, more than she was. Or something like that. She was saying it like it was an advantage I had, but I sensed she thought it was a failing. Like I was a sellout or something."**

**"Oh," Linda said, "she must have been talking about Walt."**

Mlongo hesitated. "Well, it was a general statement…but yes, if I remember right it might have been Walt that was used as an example. Anyway, she got me thinking."

Linda reflected for a minute. "I think I understand Hellen."

"You know Hellen?" he asked.

"No, not really. But what you said got me thinking of my own stuff. Of course there's Walt. I know him, and I know he talks too much. He's not just pushy with Kenyans, he's pushy with everyone. But I mean this thing about putting up with stuff that's bad, getting used to it. I don't know if things are getting worse here, or if I'm just getting older and can't handle it anymore. I'm just finding it harder and harder to function in these systems that don't function. Like government hospitals. But it seems I'm trapped in that sort of work."

Mlongo half grinned. "Well, right now you're not trapped in government work. We're both trapped here."

She gave a snort of laughter, in which he joined after a moment.

# Revolt

## 1

SEVERAL MONTHS AFTER her lunch with Mlongo, Hellen left her house to walk to work. She had spent the morning at her home, working on the history of disease screening as background for a report she was compiling on the NMPSP; the internet connection was better at home than at her office.

She usually walked through an old colonial residential area. These were houses with yards and huge eucalyptus trees, with fences or walls, and broken glass cemented into the tops of the walls, houses with large dogs that growled if you paused by the gate, and barked if you knocked. These were houses where Indian merchants now lived, and Kenyan politicians, and some of the School of Medicine professors.

Today she took a different route, shorter but noisier, near the estates. As she approached the estates, she saw a rapidly swelling crowd on the side of the street, surrounding an intense argument. She stopped on the opposite side of the road. Some neighborhood people were arguing with some professional-looking people carrying shoulder bags. Then the shoving began, and she heard, "*Bas, bas*. OK, fine. We're going," and the professional people extracted themselves from the crowd and walked away. Hellen noted the NMPSP logos on their bags.

She bought a *Nation* at the entrance to the School of Medicine and tossed it facedown on her desk. Then she picked it up again. On the back page was the headline "Refugees Reject Prevention," above a file photo of a Dadaab refugee camp packed with rows of white UNHCR tents. The article focused on a Kenyan government program intended to provide quality preventive care to all within the borders of Kenya, even refugees, in a tent-to-tent campaign. But a *Nation* reporter had learned that the people at the Dadaab camps were not happy with the program, and had been refusing to participate. Hellen skimmed to the last paragraph, and found the zinger: "'They are just looking for excuses to send us back to Somalia,' said Abdul Mohammed Noor through a translator. 'And when they take our blood, how do we know they are not injecting us with the AIDS virus?'"

She tossed the paper onto the desk again, shaking her head. Straightening her blouse, she walked down the hall to KK's office to show him her draft of the first evaluation report of the NMPSP. KK—Kiprop Kamau—was the School of Medicine's director of research. It was a dicey name, especially during the post-election violence when the Kiprops were burning the houses of the Kamaus in Eldoret, and the Kamaus were rooting out the Kiprops in Naivasha. Partly because of his no-place mixed-tribe name, but mostly because he wasn't poor, KK lived in a different space, an academic space, and navigated the equally dicey field of international research. His office bore witness: one bookshelf was filled with ring binders of research regulations, another with binders of research reports. His walls were plastered with graphs and conference announcements. He looked up as she entered: a small, animated man with a goatee. Hellen handed him the report.

Among the myriad numbers, she had underlined in red the refusal rates. KK, skimming the numbers, said, "Look at these refusal rates! Well, of course you already did," and then he started mumbling aloud the numbers he was reading. "Did you do an average for the whole program?"

"Yes, but I didn't include it because this is just a preliminary report. As of now, it's running close to fifty percent."

"So what's going on? Not that you know yet, but what *might* be going on? Well, I suppose that's what we need to find out. But a hypothesis—do you have a hypothesis? Is there a correlation between refusal rate and location? You think it's cultural? Or poor technique of presentation?"

Hellen smiled. "KK, does your mind ever stop? Even at night?"

"Oh yes, I sleep well—except when I'm working on a project. Which I guess I always am. As long as I have a pen and some cards next to my bed I'm OK—so if I have a thought, I write it down, then I go right back to sleep. Except if I have another thought. Then I write that one down—and go back to sleep."

Now Hellen was laughing. "And then you bring those cards here?"

"Oh yes," said KK, quite seriously, and produced from his shirt pocket half a dozen index cards with scribbles on both sides. "Look, here's one—"

But Hellen was laughing too loudly to hear, and after a moment KK joined in, though he wasn't exactly sure what they were laughing at.

"KK," she said, "you've got half of our next study already figured out."

"Well," he said, "we need to crunch the numbers—but it's obvious people just aren't buying this mass screening."

"Right. In fact, on the way in just now, I passed by the estates, and it looked like some NMPSP enumerators were getting hassled by the people there. We could start with a focus group right here in town, then maybe one in a low-refusal place, and two in high-refusal places, in order to flesh out some of those hypotheses you mentioned."

## 2

Dr. Alan Hodges's most noticeable physical characteristic was his receding chin. But, though his chin was receding, *he* was certainly not, even if most of his medical school classmates were now retiring. He was an American infectious-disease specialist who had been associated with the AIDS Institute since its inception—in fact, he'd incepted it, as he was fond of saying. For many years he had divided his time between his Columbia University teaching post and the Institute, but had come back to Kenya only infrequently since Mlongo had taken over as director. He remained vitally concerned with the Institute, however, creating new financial links and greasing the old ones, enjoying a rest from his frequent intercontinental trips. This was his first time back in a year.

When Mlongo came to his office that morning, he found the door open and Dr. Hodges sitting at his desk. "Leonard," Hodges said as he stood. "My goodness, I'm at your desk!" And he started to move away. "Come in and sit."

"No, no, I'm fine, Dr. Hodges," Mlongo said. "You stay there. It was your chair for far longer than it's been mine."

"Well, sit down then, and let me fill you in on some new developments," Hodges said as he returned to Mlongo's desk. "Oh, but first I must tell you what a privilege it's been for me to come back in for this surprise visit and get a look at your work. It's impeccable. Everything here is in order—better than I expected."

"Thank you, Dr. Hodges. There are some new developments?"

"Damn straight, Leonard. We're expanding. The donors like us, so we'll be expanding from being just an AIDS Institute to being a Chronic Disease Institute. Look at the synergies. We've shown we can take care of AIDS, so why can't we do the same with all chronic diseases? Heart failure, diabetes, cancer, kidney disease… And to scale up more quickly, we're creating a consortium of American universities willing to partner with us."

"Okaaay…" Mlongo sat on the upholstered chair where he usually put his guests and stared at Hodges.

"*And*, your work coordinating the mission and NGO wing of that massive screening program—what do you call it, the MPS?"

"NMPSP."

"That's it. National screening. The obvious beginning of chronic disease care."

"It looks like we will be very much in line with the latest in global health thinking—and financing—" Mlongo began, or intended to begin. It was his introduction to a response to his mentor, an affirmation of what was undoubtedly true, a fact that had different sides, different interpretations.

But Hodges was not discussing, he was announcing. "Exactly," he told Mlongo. He put his elbows on the desk and pointed his index fingers like pistols. "And all these new developments will enable us to remain in the forefront. We've got a lot of work ahead of us. What time is it now? Oh gosh, I'm late for a conference call with the US West Coast members of the consortium. It's late evening there, you know."

As he dashed out he swung the door shut. The sudden wind brushed Mlongo's face and ruffled the papers on his desk.


## 3


Dr. Walter Jorgensen was also back. This was his sixteenth trip to Evangel Mission Hospital in the last decade, including the year-long stay just after his post-graduate training. He had been bitten by the global health bug during a four-week elective late in medical school, and—as he told it every time he spoke in a church in Wisconsin—the resulting "infection" (he marked the quotes with his fingers) was lifelong. His wife, Anne, said it was like leprosy—only instead of entering a crowd crying "Unclean!" he'd enter crying "Global health!"

Before the NMPSP had started, Walt spent most of his time at Evangel Hospital, filling in for long-term missionary doctors who were on leave. Now, his vision grew in tandem with the NMPSP. He convinced himself it would be the solution for the general decline in funding from American churches for mission hospitals. And since the coordination of mission hospital NMPSP screening programs was at the AIDS Institute and the School of Medicine, he decided to go in person.

He borrowed a Toyota Land-Cruiser Prado from one of the American doctors at Evangel, and left at one p.m. the next day to ensure he wouldn't be driving after dark. The first hour was on some of Kenya's finest highways: newly redone, with wide shoulders and a passing lane on every hill. They had even started to paint the lines on the road. Walt began to picture himself touring the School of Medicine, then showering—all before dinner.

But after that first hour, the picture faded. The fine new road was blocked by a dump-truck load of gravel in his lane, with a hand-painted sign that said DIVERSION and an arrow pointing left. Several lorries in front of him had slowed and were lurching off the highway onto an unpaved dirt track. He rolled up his window because of the dust, switched on the air conditioner, and followed. The track was parallel to the highway, which appeared to be finished—but for some reason traffic was not allowed on it. He was glad he was driving a vehicle with suspension meant for this sort of road.

Twenty minutes later the diversion routed him back

onto the old highway. It was clear why the highway was being remade. The potholes looked like bomb craters, and in some places the edges of the road had been chipped off and the shoulders washed away, leaving a two-foot drop from the road to the shoulder.

Walt checked his watch. He was doing fine—or would be if this stretch was short. It wasn't; an hour later he was still creeping along the potholed road, in heavy traffic. He tried once or twice to pass the lorry in front of him—difficult enough because traffic was heavy both ways—but there was no clear road ahead. He realized his turnoff was just a few kilometers farther, so he stayed in line.

At the turnoff, he was surprised by a road free of potholes, with no vehicles going either way, and he began making up for lost time. But three minutes later he saw a long line of traffic ahead. He pulled into the passing lane, but even this second lane slowed down and eventually stopped. People ahead of him had gotten out of their cars; a few had climbed the embankment to his left.

He stuck his head out his window and asked a passerby what was wrong. There was an accident ahead, he was informed. A lorry had flipped over and was blocking the road. No, someone else said, it was a bus, with many casualties. No, an overloaded *matatu* had collided with a lorry. And no, nothing had been cleared from the road.

For two hours, Walt waited and worried. A siren

wailed behind him, but didn't seem to be getting closer. He checked his watch every five minutes and his pulse every ten. When his pulse reached ninety-five he began slow, deep breathing, preparing for the dash after the wreck was cleared to arrive at the School of Medicine just before dark. Then it started raining.

By the time the rain stopped the sun was low in the sky, and if the lorry—or whatever it was—could be pulled off the road, he thought he might be able to arrive before dark. Eventually he began to hear car engines starting up again, and the clogged traffic began to move. Finally, Walt thought, we can go—but untangling the two lines of traffic headed each way on the two-lane highway in the twilight led to plenty of honking, start-stop-starting, and frayed nerves. By the time the traffic was moving smoothly, he realized he had never seen the site of the accident.

Now the road was fairly good—except that there were no lines painted on the highway, and oncoming traffic aimed their headlights at Walt's eyes. He slowed down, leaned forward, and concentrated. By eight p.m., tense and exhausted, Walt drove into the Christian Guest House three blocks from the School of Medicine, took a cold shower, had rice and chicken, and went to bed.

*

By eight thirty the next morning he was marching down the polished red concrete floors of the School of Medicine. "Good morning," he greeted the secretary. "I have an appointment with Prof G for eight thirty."

"He is not in yet," she said, smiling. "Please have a seat."

"When do you expect him?"

"He is usually here by now; you will be the first to see him when he arrives."

Twenty minutes passed.

"Excuse me," Walt said to the secretary, standing and going over to her desk. "I wonder if you could call to see if Prof has been delayed."

She called. "He says he has been detained and will be here in thirty minutes."

"Thank you. I'll come back in half an hour." And Walt left. He didn't know the School of Medicine well, so he decided to explore. He continued down the corridor where Prof G's office was: the lighting was dim, the office doors were closed, and all he could hear were his own footsteps, echoing off the polished floor and plastered concrete walls. He turned right at the end where the corridor jogged. Suddenly, a door three meters ahead of him opened, and what seemed to be the entire first-year class burst into the corridor, coming toward him, all talking simultaneously. He backed against the wall as they passed. Three minutes later the cacophony of the students subsided, and he was left with the echoing of his own steps.

When the thirty minutes were up, Walt was back at Prof G's office. "Oh, hello again, Daktari," said the smiling secretary. "Prof still isn't back. Have a seat."

Twenty minutes later, Walt was again standing. "I think maybe I'll check back again later," he said.

"Do you have a message for the Prof?"

"Just tell him… No, I'll connect with him somehow." And Walt walked out. Where to now? He was assuming Prof G would have connected him with those at the School who could help him help the mission hospitals get a bigger piece of the NMPSP pie. But the morning was rapidly fading, and he had to get the borrowed Prado back by dark. Ah, this is Africa, he reminded himself. Calm down.

He decided to go looking for a cup of coffee, which, he told himself, would be hard to find since Kenyans do not drink coffee "culturally." The conversation with himself was silent, but his fingers still inserted the quotes around "culturally" as he walked. While passing through the parking lot, he spotted Prof G standing in a small group of people, talking and laughing. His eyes, as usual, gleamed as if it were his birthday; his woolly white hair was bushy.

He walked up to the group. Prof looked at him and

smiled. "Hello, Walt. Now, we have an appointment this morning, don't we?"

"Yes, we did," said Walt. "Um, do you have any time now?"

"Sure." Prof G moved away from the group. "You wanted to talk about the consortium?"

"Well, yes. It turns out I'm connected with one of the partners in the consortium—the University of Wisconsin—and I think we might have something unique to offer. You know the NMPSP—a great program, by the way—will likely uncover a lot of people with chronic diseases."

"Yes." Prof nodded.

"This is where I think we at Wisconsin might really shine. What I'd like to introduce, once this consortium gets going, is postgraduate training in family medicine here at the School of Medicine. Now, today I just want to plant the idea—I don't need an answer yet or anything. But I want to put a foot in the door, as we say, to kind of register my proposal early on. This is something I'd be very interested in working with you on."

"OK," Prof said. "Fine. So when the consortium becomes operational, let's put this on the table for discussion."

"Prof, that's music to my ears. Thanks so much."

Prof waited.

"Well, I guess that's really all that I wanted to do, today at least," Walt said after a moment. "To just let you guys know that I'll be around some more when this consortium is up and running."

Walt walked back to the Prado, pleased with having finally connected with Prof G, only to remember as he started the engine that he had forgotten to discuss mission hospitals and the NMPSP. Which had been the main purpose of his trip. Fiddlesticks!

It was nearing noon. As he drove out of the School of Medicine and past the entrance to the hospital, he found himself caught in what he assumed was the traffic jam from picking up and dropping off patients. But after a few minutes of waiting motionless, he heard the swelling shouting and chanting of a crowd. Several people jogged past him in the direction of the noise. He rolled down his window and asked passersby what was going on. The first person didn't know; the second ignored him. The third was happy to be an authority. A woman had just died in the hospital, he was informed. He knew that mourners could be loud and energetic, but this seemed excessive. What had happened? But his informant had left to find out.

Before long, the vanguard of the crowd came out through the hospital gate shouting, though he couldn't make out the words. As they flooded onto the street, weaving through the stopped traffic, they started kicking the cars. Three or four would stand beside a car and rock it, shouting. Walt rolled up the window of the Prado, locked his doors, and glanced behind him: blocked in. Again. As they came past him, the chants of *"Mzungu! Mzungu!"* started, and a group of young men surrounded the Prado, rocking and kicking it. Walt cowered in his seat, hands on either side of his face, praying that the glass would hold; that he wouldn't be dragged from his seat. He had a sudden vision of his bloodied body on the tarmac.

More people surged from the hospital compound, wailing as well as shouting, and the street was now so full of people that even the protesters had trouble moving. The group around his car was having a hard time rocking it because of the throngs, and finally they gave up. For twenty minutes the crowd vented, chanting in their vernacular.

Gradually the crowd thinned, and the traffic started moving. When his car was finally going at a speed faster than someone could run, Walt rolled down the window. His shirt was soaked in sweat. The crowd had gone the opposite way from his route out; there was no evidence of anything abnormal in town. Walt drove back to Evangel, confused and rattled, hoping he'd find no more lorries stretched across the road.

## 4

Until the new expanded Chronic Disease Institute could become operational, Mlongo was still director of the AIDS Institute; and as director, he was the coordinator of the activities of the NMPSP—NGO Sector. It was in that capacity, about two weeks after his discussion with Dr. Hodges, that Mlongo walked into the amenities ward of the Teaching Hospital to visit Boniface Odhiambo. Odhiambo, twenty-four years old, had been admitted the day before. Both his forearms were in casts, he had a bandage around his head, and an IV line was still running in his foot. He'd been beaten up while conducting an interview for the NMPSP.

Mlongo introduced himself and offered his profound sympathy, which Odhiambo accepted, saying he had begun to recover. Mlongo then carefully raised the question of how he happened to be in the hospital. Odhiambo was more than willing to tell him.

"*Wacha nakuambia*. We were two on my team, myself and Consolata Kinyanjui, and we had already completed three interviews that morning. It was yesterday, *sndiyo*? So we came to this house…OK, it was an hour from here and a half hour from the closest tarmac road. Right from the start we didn't have a good feeling about it, *kulikuwa kitu kibaya*; and the people seemed very suspicious, which was unusual for these rural people. We thought that maybe we needed to *kueleza* carefully, you know, *pole pole*, because maybe they didn't understand. So Connie actually started telling them about screening and why it was important, *kila kitu walitu* explain *kwenye* workshop when we see people who are hesitant."

"So you didn't insist that they accept the screening?" Mlongo clarified.

"No, no, we didn't force anything. *Hatuweze ku*force. In fact, Connie was just coming to the point whereby we tell people it is voluntary, *kila mtu apendavyo*—and although we don't have any incentives for them, the screening itself was free and so the test results *yenyewe* in most cases were like an incentive. So this lady we were talking to, she didn't smile at all and looked almost angry. She had two small kids with her, and then in the back room we heard a man's voice that kept grunting or grumbling whenever Connie would say something. But still the woman wasn't saying anything, and the two little kids looked scared, and when I stretched out my hand to the, the, the little boy he screamed and jumped back behind the woman.

"So we, me and Connie, we decided it was probably time to just check the box that says 'Refused—No reason given' and just thank them for their time, when the man in the back room *akaingia. Macho yake yalikuwa* red *kabisa, na alivyoingia ame*stagger—or I thought he staggered, but maybe he just tripped when he came in. At first he didn't say anything, he just stared at us. So I told him—I was very calm—I told him that we were from the, from the, from the screening program, and then I was going to tell him that they were very free to refuse, but before I could he started shouting, some was in his vernacular, some in Swahili, and what I got was that this particular woman was his sister and she was watching his, his, you know his kids because his wife had just died—died here at the Teaching Hospital, he said. Shouldn't have died, he said. *Watu wa hospitali, wanatudharau,* they despise us *aliweza kusema.* He brought her to Casualty bleeding—all he said was bleeding, I don't know where she was bleeding, and the first thing they asked him for was money. He said he had none but his wife was bleeding.

"Now, he didn't tell this story in order like this. I'm just trying to put together all the things he was shouting. He said his wife was sick and needed help, but no doctor came even to see her. Somebody asked him for *kitu kidogo,* something small, you know, but he said he had nothing. For two hours, he said, maybe three hours he waited with his wife but no one came. He stayed by his wife, who told him she was getting weaker. So then he went into the hospital himself to find a nurse or doctor or anyone to just see his wife, but no one came. Then she passed out, *akazimia kabisa,* and again he tried to get someone to see her, and still no one came. And then right there, in the Teaching Hospital, she stopped breathing, and no one did anything, and she died.

"So he was very angry now, you know? *Akakasirika sana.* So Connie and I told him *pole sana* and tried to say we understood, but that really got him angry, and he said how could we understand if we spent all our time looking for diseases in people who felt fine, and when people are dying and everyone knows they are dying, they just get ignored? He was waving his *fimbo* around by now and when he raised the *fimbo* to hit me, I put up my arms to protect my head, like this, and he smashed down so many times and got my arms and got my head anyway. So by this time Connie and his sister were trying to tell him to calm down and he lifted the whatever at Connie and I told her to run while I somehow rolled toward him—I was on the floor by now—and I bumped into him and he started hitting me instead on my back. And then, I don't remember much, but I think Connie and the sister got some neighbors and I guess they pulled him off me, and then they got me here."

"So this man that beat you," Mlongo said, "he didn't have any religious reason for refusing? He didn't think he'd get AIDS from our tests; he didn't have any traditional beliefs that made him refuse?"

"OK, if he had any he didn't tell me," Odhiambo answered. "He was just so angry, so angry…"

"And so beating you really had nothing to do with the screening—or did it?"

"Well, like I say, he was shouting that we were

wasting our time, like we should have been working in the hospital instead or something, I don't know. But no, he didn't say much about the screening itself."

"Now, let me ask you this, Odhiambo: do you think if he'd had some good health education before you came—if he'd heard about the screening on the radio, if he'd been to community meetings where it had been explained—do you think things would have been different?"

"You know, Doc, that man was so angry about his wife dying, he kept saying *'Wanatudharau' na mambo kama haya*. I think more education about our program would be a great thing, I think we need it. But I doubt it would make any difference for that fellow."

On his way out of the amenities ward, Mlongo found Prof G in a deep conversation with a short, elderly man wearing a sweat-stained shirt, soiled trousers, and Wellington boots. The man was jabbing his left palm with his right index finger, and though Prof tried to answer, the man had not completed his case. Mlongo heard "tractor" and *"gunia,"* and was about to pass by when Prof G flagged him. The short man held his peace while Prof stepped briefly toward Mlongo. "I'm a farmer too, you know," he started, "and I am bargaining. I trust you saw Odhiambo?"

"I'm just coming from there," said Mlongo. "You heard his story?"

"I heard about it. When the wife died, it was several days ago, I think, there was a lot of commotion here.

Did you hear about that? Traffic was blocked, and there was a big angry crowd, chanting and kicking the cars in the jam."

"Yes, I remember, but I didn't make the connection. So that was the same situation that got Odhiambo in trouble?"

"That's right," said Prof. "And this is only the beginning. You watch." And he went back to his bargaining.

5

Linda, now back at St. Anthony's, had heard about what Kasamani called the "little trouble" with some of the screening. But, she reflected happily, it wasn't *her* little trouble; she had plenty to do to keep her from looking for any other "trouble." Shortly after St. Anthony's had reopened, the referrals had started coming from the District—sometimes with notes like "Blood o/s" or "Anesthetist unavailable" or "Theater being renovated," but often with no note at all. Some patients came on their own, and told the nurses at St. Anthony's that they had gone to the District and were advised to go straight to St. Anthony's. Linda's feelings of guilt about abandoning the District abated rapidly as she realized she was still doing the work of the District. And now she found Kasamani remarkably available for help with surgery.

Well, maybe it wasn't remarkable. He had become

quite involved in the NMPSP, first as the project coordinator at the District, then as liaison between the District and St. Anthony's screening program, and finally as coordinator of the joint St. Anthony's–District partnership, a unique model of government, mission, and Dutch cooperation. With Dutch support for training, and plenty of money to pay the house-to-house screeners and their transport, the program grew rapidly. Kasamani used St. Anthony's for his headquarters, so he was available…even for surgery.

And there did seem to be provision for patient subsidy for those who could not afford the St. Anthony's rates. In the first month, Mieke van der Stoeckle oversaw the program, interviewing every patient who requested reduced fees, and "many," Linda was told, were assisted. By the end of her month, Mieke had trained someone in the finance office to continue the program. Linda was getting busier, and had no reason to follow the program closely.

<h1 style="text-align:center">6</h1>

After Mercy Onyango finished washing Linda's dishes one Monday morning, followed by her laundry, she mopped the floors, dusted the end tables and book-cases, used a long-handled feather duster to sweep the cobwebs from the ceilings, and was almost done washing the windows when Linda finally came home at two.

"Mercy, you are still here? That's great—I hardly get to see you anymore."

"Oh, I am just finishing. How are you?"—this in English. Half of the time they conversed in Swahili, half in English. Mercy took her cue from the way Linda started.

"Ah, I'm a little tired. I just don't have the energy I had when you started working for us. You know, I'm getting near sixty…"

"The work at St. Anthony's is busy?"

"It is—and I guess I like it when I think I'm being useful. But what about you? How have you been doing?"

"Oh, I'm fine," Mercy said, followed by an unspoken "but," which Linda was not too tired to notice.

"Mercy, sit down. Let's have some *chai* together."

Mercy set the kettle on while Linda got out the cups and sugar. The early afternoon sun cast the shadow of the window vine onto the table. When the tea was ready they sat opposite each other, stirring in their sugar until every grain had dissolved, watching the shadows of the vine leaves dance.

"So, you are getting near sixty," Mercy said, "and I am forty-five. You know my firstborn has finished college and has two children." She sipped her tea. "The others are…well, one is in college studying finance, one is in secondary, and one in standard six."

"So you practiced good child spacing."

"I guess we did." Another pause. "You know that new program they have, where they test people for different diseases? The NMS something?"

"Yes, the NMPSP."

"Yes, that's the one. Do you think that is a good program?"

Linda put down her cup. "It depends what you mean by good. You mean do they do a good job? Or do you mean is it important?"

"No, no, I want to know if the answers—you know, the results they give you—are good."

"You mean accurate?"

"Yes, that's it. Are the results accurate?"

Linda relaxed. "Yes, I'd say they are very accurate. Why do you ask?"

"Well, you know they came to all of our houses, and they said my blood pressure was a little high."

"Do you remember what the numbers were?"

"I think one was one hundred forty, and the other ninety."

Linda frowned. "That is borderline. Did they say anything else was wrong?"

"Yes, actually they did. They told me I had a touch of diabetes."

"A *touch* of diabetes?"

"Yes, they did a blood test—I told them I had just eaten, but they said with this test it didn't matter—and they said my sugar was starting to go up."

"Do you remember the number?"

"I think they said it was almost six."

Linda exhaled deeply. "Oh my goodness. OK, I see what's going on—or I think I do. What those guys were measuring were *risk factors*, maybe the very earliest signs of diseases. That doesn't mean you *have* high blood pressure or diabetes, but that you might be getting them."

"Yes, they said something like that. So, last week some of them came back to our place for follow-up, and they said I should definitely be checked in one of their new clinics. I don't understand it all, but these clinics are somehow connected with the AIDS Institute." Mercy stared into her tea cup. "High blood pressure and diabetes…are they…are they part of AIDS?"

Linda reached across the table and took Mercy's hand. "No, Mercy, there is no connection between them. The only thing is that they are all chronic diseases, meaning they last a long time—so some of the ways we approach them are similar. Not the drugs, but you know, helping people *take* their drugs every day. Stuff like that. But the thing is, you don't really have high blood pressure or diabetes. At least not yet."

"You don't think I need to go to one of those new clinics?"

"Tell you what, Mercy. Let me take your blood

pressure right now, and then we'll know if you need to go." She went over to the cabinet and rooted in a drawer for a blood pressure cuff and stethoscope. Mercy stared at the trembling shadow of the vine, which was shifting as the sun dropped. Linda returned and took Mercy's pressure. "Hmm. Well, actually, it *is* up a bit now—it's one fifty over one hundred. We should check it again before you leave, but if it's still up, maybe you should go back and be checked at one of those clinics. Or, if you want, we could see you directly at St. Anthony's."

Mercy grinned shyly. "That would be nice. Could I get my ANC care there as well?"

"You're pregnant?" Linda exclaimed.

Mercy nodded.

"How far along?"

"Almost six months."

7

The next morning, the crowd Linda found at the outpatient waiting bay of St. Anthony's Hospital was not of sick people—or at least not mostly. One mother held a lethargic infant, and one young man sat with his bandaged foot propped on a bench. But there were about thirty hospital staff: white-dressed nurses, yellow-dressed cleaners, blue-dressed patient attendants, and the white-coated doctors Kasamani and Flogel—the latter the current Dutch volunteer. All were watching the news on the television. The picture was jumping and periodically lost color, and the sound alternated between harsh and muffled, but the audience was attentive.

The newscaster was interviewing a representative of the Ministry of Health, interspersed with clips of crowds of angry people around district hospitals—from the Coast, from Central Province, from Nyanza, from North and South Rift—and asking the Ministry representative to comment on the situation, and especially on the evident anger of the crowds.

"But seriously, madam," the Ministry representative was saying, "these clips you have shown hardly indicate a pattern. The only recent one was the small incident in Nyanza yesterday. And the clips taken on the Coast are from last year, if I'm not mistaken."

"But that is exactly the point we at TVNews are making," she answered. "There is widespread and long-standing discontent with government health services, which now seems to have reached a breaking point. TVNews has learned that nine district hospitals across the country are simply closed because of the disturbances, and countless others are reduced to emergency services only."

"But that is—"

"And reports coming in this morning are of wildcat strikes by hospital workers in almost every province."

"Yes, my office has been appraised of these strikes," the representative said, "and we do not take these illegal actions lightly. Those strikers risk being summarily sacked unless they demonstrate due cause."

"Oh, now that is serious," one of the white-dressed nurses said to no one in particular.

"No, this is not amusing," said another. The crowd was no longer watching the TV.

"Imagine," someone else said. "Sacking nurses when they try to express a legitimate concern—and after serious overwork on the wards."

"And what of those at the District here?"

"Surely they are fed up too."

Eventually they were all talking at once. Kasamani and his Dutch colleague headed off to the wards, and some others in the crowd began to drift away. Linda caught up with Kasamani to see what he knew.

"You haven't heard?" Kasamani asked Linda. "The nurses at the District are striking. Get ready for lots of patients here."

"What's the strike about?"

"Apparently some family members were upset about their patient's death. Yesterday but one. There was a scuffle and a nurse got knocked down—broke her wrist, I think. So the nurses say there are unsafe working conditions. It looks like we are going to be busy here at St. Anthony's."

"Striking just because a nurse broke her wrist?"

"No, that was just the trigger. Nurses are not happy—anywhere. But it's not pay this time. The origin of this strike is patients themselves, fed up because their medical care is so bad. The nurses are just following."

*

Three days later Linda *was* busy: the nurses at St. Anthony's had gone on strike in sympathy with the nurses at the District. The hospital was closed for new admissions, but there was still care for those who remained, there being nowhere to transfer them. Kasamani had disappeared. Linda and Flogel made rounds on all the patients, then tried to nurse them as well, administering medications and other treatments. By the end of the week, most had been discharged, but several remained as "discharges-in," unable to pay their bills. Linda visited the finance office and reminded them of the patient subsidy, a policy that needed to be located, dusted off, and restarted…after confirmation from Dr. Flogel that the policy was still in place, which he needed to confirm with Mieke van der Stoeckle in Holland because he had never heard of it.

Linda came home frazzled and exhausted. She put on the electric kettle for tea and lay down…just for a minute, she told herself, just until the water boiled…

By the time she woke, the boiled water was already tepid. She turned the kettle on again and checked her email, and found this from her son, Josh, in Boston:

Hi Mom. So Kenya's on the front pages again. What's going on? Sounds like post-election all over again. Is it true most of the hospitals are closed? So where does this leave you? And I just saw on Yahoo News that some of the strikes are turning violent, and that 12 people (says Yahoo) have been killed. So who takes care of those who are injured? Any violence at St. Anthony's or the District?

Love, Josh

Linda wasn't sure how to answer. She had been too busy to realize that she was about to confront another decision about St. Anthony's, less than a month after the decision that had taken her there. But what were her choices? If St. Anthony's was closed, and the District was closed, what would she do? She was confronting enforced inactivity in the middle of chaos.

## Somalia

"There he goes again."

"What?" Linda had been trying to weave twigs from the acacia tree into a cross. "There who goes again?" she asked without looking up, trying to bend the green twig without breaking it.

"The guard—the tall one. Back to the *choo*. He's been out five times just this morning. And when he comes back he doesn't look so good."

"He needs ORS." The twig she was bending snapped, and she tossed the sculpture on the ground.

"Sure, but did you bring any ORS packets? Because I'm pretty sure they don't have any here."

"Oh, you young doctors," Linda said, smiling. "Didn't you ever learn about the three-finger pinch of salt, and enough sugar to fill the palm of your hand, mixed into a cup of water?"

Mlongo thought for a minute, and then the guard came out of the *choo*, looking wretched. Mlongo called him over. The other guard stood up, waving his AK-47 and shouting, but the sick guard just fell to his knees and vomited. Mlongo, first in Swahili, and then with some Somali words, spoke to the guard with the AK, and he stopped shouting. Mlongo kept talking calmly, showing the guard his open empty hands. The guard with the AK motioned for his sick colleague to move toward Mlongo, ordering him to stop when he was two meters away.

Linda listened to the conversation. She understood the Swahili: Mlongo was explaining her homemade ORS formula to the sick guard. Then Mlongo was using Swahili words she didn't know, then more Somali words. The guard started to look interested and asked a question. Mlongo answered, and this time it sounded mostly Somali. Now the guard with the AK joined the discussion. A few minutes later they were finished.

"I didn't know you knew Somali," Linda said.

"I don't really."

"But I heard you just now. How did you learn?"

"Well, we've been hearing the guards talk with each other for over three weeks now. Haven't some of the words started to seem familiar to you?"

"Um, *no*. So what did you tell that guy? I heard you tell him about ORS, then I got lost."

"Well, as long as he stays hydrated, I suggested some herbs he could use. For some reason these young guys don't know about that."

Several hours later the sick guard came back with some leaves and some roots. Mlongo pointed to the leaves, and explained some more. The guard left.

The next morning the guard made only two trips to the choo, looking much brighter, and none in the afternoon.

"It was the homemade ORS," said Linda

Mlongo shook his head. "It was the herbs."

They both laughed.

"You do what you need to do," Linda said, and then stopped. Mlongo looked at her expectantly. She didn't want to tell him what had started roiling inside her.

# Lord Have Mercy

## 1

DURING THE STRIKE, Ng'etich came to the District Hospital every day. The first day, he passed a large crowd of nurses who had gathered in front of the hospital. He made his rounds as he always did, without a nurse accompanying him, but now there was no nurse at the desk to read his orders and distribute medicines. He went back outside to where the nurses were and stood among them, listening. A few were militant, incensed that a nurse could be injured in the line of duty—especially when that same nurse had tried to resuscitate a patient.

"And it wasn't even her fault that the patient died!"

"Surely. Why do they blame the nurses? We are with those patients all day, and we are overstretched. And what about the doctors?"

"Even them, they are not enough. Why doesn't the Ministry send us what we need—enough nurses *and* doctors?"

"And medicines!"

"Yes, of course—and IV fluids, and giving sets…"

Ng'etich noticed Salome over to his left, and squeezed through the crowd toward her.

"Hello, Daktari," she greeted him. "Are you striking too?"

Salome, fifteen years older than Ng'etich, had not begun the middle-aged, middle-body spread many of her age-mates had succumbed to. She remained trim and active—but her energy wasn't fully used in her current job. Though neither angry nor militant, she was striking.

"No, Salome, I just came from rounds. But I finished... Tell me what's been happening here."

"Daktari, something needs to change. OK, sure, a nurse was hurt, but those family members had a right to be upset..."

"That's just it," Ng'etich said. "The whole thing seems so confusing, especially the way the *Nation* reported it. Did you see that headline? 'Nurse Breaks Wrist; Union Debates National Strike.'"

"Why don't they just tell the truth, Daktari? We know these hospitals; we work here day and night. When we are sick, we and our families are admitted here. We try to work, but we have nothing to work with—we've had no insulin or penicillin for three weeks; we haven't had bleach for a month! Patients— and that means us when our families are admitted— have to buy the sterile gloves and giving sets for IVs..."

By early afternoon, many of the nurses had gone home. None came in for the evening shift, and the patients waiting for treatment left, realizing there would be no treatment that day. At seven p.m., a rowdy group of young men stormed into the hospital compound and nailed the front door of the hospital shut. They dragged old tires into the parking lot and set them alight: black acrid smoke hung in the air, and even the police stayed away.

The next morning, the police came to pry off the boards nailed to the front door and extinguish the smoldering tires. By then there were no protestors, and few patients waiting to be seen, but no one to see them. Family members carried food in to the patients left on the wards, but food was all they were getting. Ng'etich again tried to make rounds, though by now it was clear even to him that he was documenting the collapse of his health system, not ameliorating it.

By midday some of the nurses arrived in uniform, singing and chanting their demands for better working conditions. The relatives of the patient who died were also there to finally retrieve his body from the morgue. Salome, not in uniform today, went to where the relatives were, greeted them, and offered them condolences. A few relatives who recognized her as a nurse asked why she wasn't on "the other side" with her colleagues. She condoled with them again and said she didn't think there *were* sides. Yes, she was still a nurse, and was still on strike—but not against them.

Then she went back to be with the nurses, and they

wanted to know why she wasn't wearing her uniform, and if she had gone to "the other side." She explained that she hadn't come to work today and so didn't need her uniform; she also explained, again, that she didn't think there were sides, and that what the nurses and relatives both wanted was better care for patients. By the time the relatives had collected *marehemu*, the deceased, and were moving in procession out of the hospital compound, many of the nurses had joined them, singing church songs. Ng'etich stood by watching, then returned to his quarters within the compound.

That evening, when the temperature dropped, the protests heated up again: several of the young men came back drunk, nailed the door shut again, and burned more tires. This time the police came late in the evening, but by then the young men were gone.

*

The third day of the strike the nurses came back to strike, along with more angry townspeople—this time supporting the nurses. The crowd was larger and noisier than the day before, and their protests were impassioned. But there was no one there to protest against. Ng'etich came out again, listening and watching.

A young mother who had come in from a village with her baby stopped in the parking lot when she saw the crowd. It confused her: she had come to get her baby treated, but there was no queue, there were no other patients. She turned this way and that in confusion, and then saw Ng'etich standing by the steps to the hospital in his white coat, the stethoscope around his neck. She threaded her way through the crowd, held her baby out to Ng'etich, and started crying. The child was unconscious, and the woman said he had been having convulsions.

Ng'etich took her aside, under a tree, and did a quick examination. He told her he had no access to a lab, but the child likely had malaria. He suggested the chemist across the street for the appropriate malaria treatment, and when the mother said she had come with no money, he gave her one hundred shillings for the drug. While he was still under the tree, two other mothers came with their babies, and before they left, an old man came wanting advice for a medicine refill.

In the evening the young jobless men came back, but before they had gotten started nailing and burning, the police arrived and fired a tear-gas canister at them. Ng'etich, watching from his home in the hospital compound, saw the young men scatter. The police, wearing gas masks and armed with truncheons, swung at each fleeing protester. Several of the young men managed to run away, some limping or cradling broken arms, their escape ensured because most of the police had gathered around one easy target, now beaten unconscious. The police loaded him into their vehicle and rattled off.

Ng'etich walked to the front of the hospital. One of the young men who had been beaten had hidden behind the hospital, and after the police left he came out, bleeding from a deep gash in his head. Ng'etich tied the boy's shirt around his head to slow the bleeding, then went in a back door of the hospital to find some gauze, gloves, sutures, and a few sterile instruments. The boy refused to follow him into the hospital, so he found an outside water tap, cleaned the wound, and sutured it closed.

The next morning, the crowd started gathering even earlier, protesting now about the beating of the youths the previous night. There were rumors that the one the police had taken away had died. Some TV reporters came with their video cameras to cover the protest, which became quite heated while they were there. But it was still a hospital, and people were still arriving to seek treatment. Another mother with a lethargic infant came up to Ng'etich, and as he moved back toward his tree, he found Salome beside him.

"I saw you yesterday treating patients, Daktari. You need a bench at least, and maybe this blood pressure cuff. All our thermometers are broken—but there are still some IV fluids and giving sets. Shall I bring you some?"

Ng'etich smiled. "Why not? And maybe a few vials of quinine?"

Soon half a dozen women were lined up with their

infants. Among them was a middle-aged woman with swollen legs, holding her belly. After Ng'etich and Salome had seen several of the mothers with children, the middle-aged woman moved onto the bench. She sat quietly for a moment, then told them she had belly pain. Ng'etich waited. And a headache. The woman wasn't saying much.

"Are you pregnant?"

The woman nodded.

"How far along?"

"Six months."

Salome wrapped the blood pressure cuff around the woman's arm as Ng'etich continued to get her history. She put on the stethoscope and listened—then pumped up the cuff again. Ng'etich looked at Salome. "I'm getting one eighty over one ten," she answered.

"I think you need to be in a hospital," said Ng'etich to the woman, "but ours is closed. Can you go to St. Anthony's? I believe Dr. Jankowski is working there now."

"I know—I have worked for Dr. Linda for many years. But those nurses are striking as well. St. Anthony's is closed."

"That's bad. You have to try to get to a hospital."

"Yes, Daktari." Which clearly meant "Impossible, Daktari."

"Do you think you can get to Kisumu? Or Eldoret? Or Nakuru?"

"I can try, Daktari." Meaning "That is also impossible."

"Listen: at least you need complete bed rest for now—and begin to look for some way to get to a hospital to deliver as soon as possible. And across the street at the chemist you can get some of this medicine"—he scribbled something on a slip of paper—"to help you to stay in bed, and this other one to bring your blood pressure down. These medicines are not very expensive. You have money?"

She nodded.

"And if anything happens, please come back. If I see Daktari Linda, I will tell her I've seen you. Your name?"

"Mercy. Mercy Onyango."

*

They were still seeing their last few patients in the dying light of early evening when the youths arrived again, less drunk and more heavily armed: *pangas*, *rungus*, bows and arrows. They dragged more tires into the parking lot and drenched them in petrol. Two went to the front door and again began nailing boards over it.

Unfortunately, the other side had also joined the local arms race: the GSU unit—the paramilitary wing of the police—arrived shortly after the youths. A huge khaki lorry parked outside the hospital gate, and two dozen men in camouflage fatigues jumped down, each clutching an assault rifle. Ng'etich quickly moved back from his tree toward his house in the compound, and watched from behind a car there. The GSU came into the hospital compound and ordered the young men to disburse; the young men shouted back—some from behind parked cars or bushes, most out in the open, waving their *pangas* and *rungus*, taunting the officers.

One of the GSU officers began firing his assault rifle in the air. In response, one protester threw a rock, hitting the officer in the shoulder. Half a dozen GSU began firing simultaneously, and Ng'etich flung himself down behind the car, his stethoscope pressing into his chest. But the noise was over as suddenly as it had begun. After a minute, Ng'etich rose to a crouch and looked through the window of the car: the GSU had their rifles trained on the protesters, who were standing with their empty hands raised, the bows, arrows, *rungus*, and *pangas* at their feet. To the left of the front door, beside a bush, were three bloody bodies. Half of the officers rounded up the protestors who were still alive, beating and kicking them into the lorry. The others scooped up the three dead bodies and dumped them in alongside the protestors, leaving the rest of the armed men to guard the hospital. Ng'etich sat behind the car, trying to keep his breathing quiet. He was shivering.

*

The next day the protest crowd was even larger, as was the GSU presence. Ng'etich stayed at his house throughout the morning, but the crowd in front kept chanting, and the GSU kept threatening.

In early afternoon, as he was sitting at his table sipping chai, he saw a woman with an infant walking through the crowd, coming toward the back of his house. He went to the back window: half a dozen women with their infants were sitting on the dry grass, waiting. He called Salome's cell phone, and soon their small clinic was operational in his backyard, with women coming and going—some through a small gap in his hedge, most climbing over his meter-and-a-half-high back fence.

# 2

A week later, Mlongo's office was again the scene of an international development parley. Hodges had once again claimed the desk chair, so Mlongo sat on his desk, next to the AIDS ribbon sculpture built from red pills. They were considering the implications to chronic disease care of the increasing hospital closures. They were not arguing; no, certainly not arguing. When Mlongo bemoaned the absence of acute care services for large swaths of the population, Hodges was in complete agreement. And when Hodges suggested that these closures did not need to inhibit the ongoing development of the Chronic Disease Institutes parallel to the AIDS Institute, Mlongo agreed that hostility toward public institutions did not need to spill over to private or NGO institutions. He did, however, emphasize the folly of chronic disease care without a basic health system to deliver it—which, Hodges readily granted, went without saying. However, he noted, this did not negate the changing disease *pattern*, meaning that chronic disease was a reality that Kenya must be ready for. Most certainly, Mlongo agreed, along with robust acute care. But of course, Hodges assented, they needed both, but the lack of one should not prevent the development of the other. And so they went on agreeing.

In the middle of this spirited agreement, Hellen tapped on the door and poked her head in. "You are having a meeting?"

"Dr. Nyalo! No, no." Hodges stood up. "Leonard and I were just thinking through some of the steps we need to take to get these Chronic Disease Institutes up and running. And"—he nodded to Mlongo—"the difficulty of this in the context of these hospital closures. So, what can we do for you, dear?"

"Well, *dear*," she said, leaning slightly on the word, "I was just dropping by to greet Mlongo and see how

NMPSP was going, 'in the context of all these hospital closures,' as you put it. Surely they've got to be affecting some of the screening activities."

Mlongo waited a second to see if Hodges was planning to answer, and then addressed Hellen: "Actually, a bit less than you might expect, at least from the NGO sector. Of course, we don't know about the government sector—except for the St. Anthony's–District linkage, and that one has pretty much stopped since both hospitals are closed now." He paused, weighing the merits of his next comment. "Of course it does seem that, in some places at least, NMPSP served as a catalyst for some of these, um…uprisings."

Hellen flicked her eyebrows up and stared at Mlongo, but Hodges was the one who responded. "Do you really think so, Leonard? I had heard this theory bandied about, but it was never clear to me why people feel this way. What could be the connection between offering a free screening service, and anger about poor care in some of these government hospitals?"

Hellen and Mlongo were looking at each other, trying to decide how to answer, when there was another knock on the door, and Gillian walked in.

"My goodness!" Hodges boomed from the desk chair. "Your office is like Grand Central Station, Leonard. How are you, Dr. Peel? Are you still with us?"

"Cracking, Hodges. How are you? And Hellen? Len?"

Mlongo, assuming he was the intended focus of her visit, answered, "We're fine here. What news do you bring from Dadaab?"

"Not much. You know about the high refusal rates for screening there?"

"Yes, we heard. And what about these demonstrations?" Mlongo asked. "Have they affected the medical care on those sides?"

"Not really. NGOs don't strike, you know." No one answered. "Actually, that's partly why I dropped by. You got a minute, Mlongo?"

"Sure. Shall we step out?"

"Well, actually, I'd appreciate all your thoughts. So here it is: MSF—I still keep up with them, you know—has kept pretty close tabs on all these events, and is concerned about where people are getting care with so many hospitals closed. So they're sort of wondering about setting up a field hospital in one of the densely populated areas, like Nyanza or Western or Central. What do you think?"

The three looked back and forth at each other, but no one spoke.

"What? You're all acting like I just proposed setting up a brothel."

Hellen cleared her throat. "You mean one of those portable hospitals they use in wars? A…what do they call it in the States, a MASH hospital? In the middle of Kenya?"

"Well, not a MASH. We're not talking about war wounded. I mean just a regular hospital for sick people. OK, maybe it could be set up in a school, you know. Or if not, maybe MSF would have to bring in some tents or something. But that's not the point."

"OK," Mlongo tried, "what is the point?"

"It's simple, isn't it? With all these hospitals closed, what are all those severely ill people doing, the ones who would otherwise be hospitalized? I don't get what you guys don't get. I mean, they're dying, right?"

Hellen again: "I'm sure some are; some would die anyway. But it's interesting you ask about what people are doing now that so many hospitals are closed. I had exactly the same question—you know the Teaching Hospital is closed too—so the other day a couple of the medical students and I went around some of the estates, just asking people we met. Randomly, you know, it wasn't an official study or anything. You know what we found?"

"Do tell."

"First—and we expected this—there were complaints, and since we were from the School of Medicine, they assumed we were trying to set up something. But when they realized we were just asking, and had nothing to give them, but we really were interested in how they were dealing with the crisis, and what they saw people doing who were sick, they started talking. And mostly they said they prayed, or asked someone to pray. So we asked them if that was helpful. Did it work? And of course there wasn't just one answer, but quite a few said they had seen people who got better. I don't know what was wrong with them, but these people we talked to all seemed to pray.

"Then we pushed a bit more. We asked if they used local herbal medicine. Some of them would laugh bashfully. But yes, they would often admit, they used herbs. And so we asked: did they, or their relatives, get better when they used herbs? And again, like with prayer, quite a few admitted that herbs worked."

Gillian and Hodges listened skeptically, waiting for the science. Mlongo said, "Very interesting, Hellen. You know, that might be worth developing into a formal study."

"We're actually thinking of that," said Hellen.

Hodges put a large hand on the desk. "Now, wait. Dr. Peel here has raised a very good question. OK, maybe we don't need a field hospital—you actually came just to ask, didn't you?—but her proposal does deserve a reasoned answer, not just anecdotes. Do we have any morbidity and mortality statistics since these hospitals have closed?"

"Those will, of course, be available," Hellen answered, "but it takes time to see a real trend, and sometimes we only see one in retrospect. I wouldn't act on a blip one way or the other in mortality stats. We'd have no way of knowing what caused it."

"Fair enough," said Hodges, "but that still begs the

question. Do you have a crisis that requires some outside help, or not? Should MSF come in? Or is this the time to put out a plea to the consortium members? We haven't officially started yet, but this might be a great opportunity to introduce some of the US universities to the situation here—and give them practical experience as well, especially the students and residents. But in the meantime, and I think Leonard here will agree with me, the AIDS Institute at least will be ensuring that no one goes without their ARVs. It's also a lesson—I can see this now—to be very careful about linking our new chronic disease efforts too closely to the government health system."

"Fine, fine," said Gillian, "but what about the field hospital? What shall I tell MSF?"

"Oh," said Hellen, "if they want to set up a field hospital, I think they should go ahead and do that."

"As long as they coordinate with the government," Mlongo added. "I know it's Doctors *Without* Borders, but we still have our borders here, and there's no rebel group claiming new borders. Maybe the government will welcome MSF, but maybe they'll be embarrassed to let them in. I don't know."

"Well, thanks guys." Gillian started to leave. But she turned around in the doorway, her face flushed. "I...I—" she stammered. "You know, I just don't get it. You guys stand around and talk about prayers and herbs and government borders and practical experience for American students and shit like that, and your damn hospitals are closed. Bloody hell, Congo and Somalia have better health systems than you do right now." She stopped. No one even tried to respond. "Well, at least I'm going to move *my* arse!" And she bolted out the door.


# 3


A month after seeing Ng'etich under the tree outside the hospital, Mercy felt terrible. She sat down and put her feet up on a stool: her legs were more swollen than they had been earlier that morning. Her headache was worse, and she couldn't see well. She knew she needed to go back to that kind doctor at the District, but she didn't feel like traveling. She felt her baby kick—but just after that she noticed nausea. OK, she would go to the District Hospital; even if that doctor couldn't admit her, at least he would tell her what was going on. She stood to go, but before she could make it outside she threw up. She sat back down. She needed to clean it up, but now instead of nausea she felt pain in her belly. Putting her hand on the doorframe, she tried to get to her feet, but speckles of light swarmed…

She woke up groggy, and opened her eyes to see the burgundy stripe at the base of the wall. She was lying on the floor. Her head…she raised her hand to touch her forehead…something sticky. Her hand came away red. She drifted, and woke again to the sour, pungent smell of vomit. She needed to clean it up—but why was she on the floor? And where had the blood on her hand come from? The baby kicked again. She tried to sit up, but her head was pounding.

Sometime later—it might have been minutes or hours—she heard a familiar voice. "Hey, who threw up in here?" Her son Joshua, the one in secondary school. Then the tone changed. "Mum, what are you doing on the floor—and why is your head bleeding? Mum, what happened to you?" And he knelt down next to her.

"I don't know. My head…"

"Yes, you have a cut on your head. Don't touch it. We need to get you to the hospital."

"But it was hurting before…"

When she woke up again, a neighbor was holding her arms, and there was a spoon in her mouth; she spat blood. She heard Joshua again: "Here, let's bring her out. The *piki-piki* is on the way coming." She was aware of being lifted onto the back of a motorcycle in pouring rain, straddling the seat, propped between the driver in front of her and her son behind. "District Hospital," Joshua said, and they sped off.

<br>

## 4

Linda and Ng'etich were both exhausted. The District Hospital was officially closed—and although community protests were the reason the Ministry had closed the hospital, community penury was the reason Ng'etich kept working there. Ng'etich had gotten permission to organize a walk-in clinic at the Casualty Ward, and as soon as Linda found out, she asked if she could join him. Several Ministry nurses, among them Salome, chose to help. All retained their Ministry paychecks—and while the Ministry praised their initiative, their praise did not extend to running expenses. It was temporary anyway, until the government sorted out a way to reopen the hospitals.

There was no anesthetist, no functioning operating theater, no functioning laboratory, no inpatients. Ng'etich and Linda had access to what was left in the pharmacy, much of it now used up. The only fees they charged were for the supplies they used—sutures, gauze, IVs, needles, tubing, gloves, antiseptics. Enough people valued their efforts that their supply of those essentials remained just about constant. They treated what they could and sent patients to the local pharmacies in town for medications. Those needing hospitalization—and there were many every day—were left on their own to find transport to a private one. Occasionally, Linda would call Gillian, who had gotten permission to set up a field hospital about forty-five minutes away, and if the MSF vehicle was nearby, it would carry people to their hospital.

One day in October, during a late-afternoon thunderstorm, a motorcycle drove up to the Casualty entrance and Mercy's teenage son jumped off the back, holding his mother upright. About fifteen people were sheltering on the veranda at the entrance, and one of them helped him lift her from the seat. Together they sloshed her through a puddle up to the door. After they set her on a bench, Joshua wandered down the hall, poking his head into each examining room. Linda looked up and saw a drenched adolescent face she knew she recognized—but from where? "Dr. Linda?" he said. "Could you please help my mother?"

"Joshua! My goodness! Where is she?"

"Right here, Dr. Linda. Please come."

Linda had just started cleaning and suturing several deep *panga* wounds on a drunk man's head, and asked Salome to go with Joshua and find out what the problem was.

Salome came back a few minutes later. "It seems like the woman has been fitting," she said. "The son observed one episode, and thinks there was another when she was alone before he got home. You know this woman?"

"Yes," Linda said, hunting for a fresh bleeder she had just exposed while cleaning the largest wound. "She works for me, more than twenty years now. What is her blood pressure?"

"Oh my," Salome said. "I saw her with Ng'etich here, last month. Let me take her pressure." And she scurried away. In five minutes she was back. "I don't know if this machine is working right, but I'm getting two hundred over one sixty."

"Wow! Does she have leg edema? Proteinuria?"

"Let me check." Salome turned, but Linda stopped her.

"No, no, I'm just thinking out loud. She's pregnant and had signs of preeclampsia, oh, more than a month ago. She's likely eclamptic. Is she seizing right now?"

"No, but she seems drowsy."

"Not good. Is Ng'etich free?"

"No, he's sorting out a girl with a severe asthma attack, and someone else was just brought in with an overdose. Unconscious."

"Lordy! Listen, Salome, can you go to the pharmacy and see if they have any magnesium sulfate there? I don't think we've used any since we've been here, so maybe they have a few vials left."

"Yes, Daktari."

Salome hurried off while Linda continued to try and stop the bleeding in the man's scalp. Fifteen minutes later, Salome returned with a dusty box. "I found this way in the back, behind some other boxes, but we never used these vials on maternity, Daktari. The Ministry sent us premixed bottles of IV mag sulfate, ready to use."

"That's OK, we can mix it here. Let me see one of the vials." Salome held up a vial and Linda read, "Magnesium sulfate one gram..." But before she finished reading, the wound in front of her filled with blood. One of the wounds was a flap, and now she had to extend the laceration to identify the bleeder. She finally found it and tied it off, and was able to dab the wound dry. "OK, Salome, could you please suture the skin on this man's scalp? I think I've gotten all the bleeders." Linda removed her gloves as Salome came around to take her place.

When Linda came out of the room, Joshua stood and came toward her; he had been sitting next to his mother on the bench where he had first deposited her. Mercy looked up and summoned a wavering smile.

"Mercy!" Linda exclaimed. "Here, let's get you into a room. What happened?"

Joshua answered. "We've tried to talk with her but she doesn't say much, only that her head hurts. I found her on the floor when I came home. She had vomited and there was that cut on her head. Then while I was there she started jerking all over—seizure, right? So I called some neighbors and we put a spoon in her mouth and tried to keep her from jerking." They helped Mercy get onto an examining table.

"That's a very helpful bit of history, Joshua. You did well in bringing her here so quickly—and in the rain, too! She probably had a seizure and bumped her head before you got home. Now let me see what I can do. Mercy, how do you feel?"

Mercy ran her tongue over her lips, and said

slowly, "My head hurts—and somehow it is bleeding. But it was hurting before I found the blood. What happened?"

"It seems you've had a seizure or two, and you probably fell on your head. Do you have pain anywhere else?"

"Yes, my stomach hurts, and I think I threw up at home. And my legs…"

Linda looked down and saw marked swelling beyond both knees. Mercy put a hand on Linda's arm. "Is my baby OK?"

"I'll be checking that in just a minute. Let me just recheck your blood pressure first; the nurse told me it was up more than when I checked it at home. So, when was the last time it was checked?" Linda asked as she wrapped the blood pressure cuff around Mercy's arm.

"When this nurse and the other *daktari* saw me a month ago."

"And what was it then?"

"I think they said one eighty over something."

Linda finished taking her pressure, confirmed what the nurse had told her, and then listened to Mercy's belly for the baby's heartbeat. "Well, I can't hear the baby's heartbeat right now, but…" Linda sat down. She closed her eyes a moment, and then looked from Mercy to Joshua and back. "OK," she said, "the first thing is to get you to a hospital where they can take good care of you and get this whole thing sorted out.

I think the best would be for me to call Dr. Peel at the new MSF hospital they've just set up—it's nearly an hour from here—and have their driver come and get you. Is that OK with you?"

"How much will that cost?" Mercy asked.

Linda was about to reassure her when Joshua spoke up. "Mum, you've got to go. We'll sort all that out later."

Linda asked Joshua to step out of the room with her while she called Gillian and asked for the MSF vehicle. Then she explained to Joshua that his mother was quite ill, but that getting her to a hospital soon would likely take care of the whole problem. They could do a C-section, take the baby out, and his mother should completely recover. Of course the baby might not survive, but the important thing was to start treatment.

"Can you start treatment here while we wait?" Joshua asked.

"Actually, I was just about to do that." They went back into the room together. "So Mercy, Dr. Peel said she is sending the driver now. While we wait, we can start some medication that will keep you from having more seizures until you get there. And I think I should put a stitch or two in that cut on your forehead."

Linda went back to the room where Salome was finishing suturing the scalp wounds to get what she needed to sew up Mercy's much smaller wound. "This is the mag sulfate?" she asked as she was leaving.

"Yes. It should be labeled."

Linda glanced at the vials, saw the "one gram," and put four vials in a bottle of dextrose.

When she came back, Joshua was bending over his mother, trying to keep her arms from jerking. "It's happening again," he said to Linda. All of Mercy's limbs were jerking rhythmically, her jaw was clenched, her mouth foaming, and her eyes had rolled up.

"It's OK, Joshua, that's what happens with seizures. It shouldn't last too long, and as soon as she stops we'll start an IV and get some of this medicine into her. That should keep any more of them from happening."

The shaking lasted another thirty seconds. As soon as the seizure was over, Linda started an IV in Mercy's arm.

"But she isn't awake yet, Dr. Linda," Joshua said.

"Most people who have seizures sleep for some time afterward. That's normal." She took Mercy's blood pressure again: 205/160; the pulse was 90. She jotted the numbers down and got out a fresh tubing for the magnesium. She wanted the loading dose to go in over half an hour, meaning it should be finished by the time the MSF vehicle arrived. Then she left Joshua with his mother while she went to find Ng'etich.

The asthma patient Ng'etich was with was still very tight, and he looked worried. He had no nebulizer, and had already used all the drugs on hand. He told Linda he wished he had some magnesium.

"Magnesium sulfate?" she asked. "You can use that for asthma?"

"Of course it's not the first drug," he answered, "but it is apparently useful for *status asthmaticus*, when other drugs aren't working. It's in the new guidelines."

"Well, Ng'etich, today I have a magic wand. You want magnesium? I'll get you magnesium," and she left, returning a minute later with the dusty box of magnesium vials. She went back to Mercy; the blood pressure was down to 180/140. Good.

"But Dr. Linda, she's not awake yet."

"Yes, Joshua, but the blood pressure is coming down. We're on the right track."

Fifteen minutes later the blood pressure was 150/100 and the pulse 60. "But Dr. Linda, she is not awake yet."

"Sometimes it takes a long time." But this was too long, Linda thought. She checked it again. The blood pressure was 120/60; five minutes later it was 100/40. "Joshua, could you find the nurse and ask her to bring some normal saline?" Yes, normal saline—but why is the pulse only 40? Come on, Mercy, wake up!

Salome came in, followed by Joshua.

"Ah, Salome," Linda said. "Thanks. Put up the saline and run it open, OK? And Joshua, could you ask Dr. Ng'etich to come in?" What was going on? Why were her hands cold? Where was her pulse? OK, there it is…I think. Breathe, Mercy, breathe. "Salome, do we have a bag and mask?"

"There should be one. Let me check."

"Ng'etich! Thanks for coming. This lady has

eclampsia. I've loaded her with mag sulfate, and the pressure came down, but it's now sixty palpable, so we started saline."

"How much blood pressure medicine did you give her?"

"None."

Ng'etich listened to her chest, then started doing external chest compressions.

"Just a second, Ng'etich." Linda gave Mercy a few breaths mouth to mouth, then nodded to Ng'etich, who continued. Salome came with the bag and mask, which Linda fastened to Mercy's face. Three chest compressions, a breath. Three chest compressions, a breath. Linda put a finger on Mercy's neck. "I'm getting a pulse with your compressions." Three more, a breath. Three more, a breath. "Do we have epinephrine, Salome?" Three more, a breath. Three more, a breath. Salome held up a vial of epinephrine. "Good," Linda said. "Give the epi."

"Linda, how are her pupils?"

Linda knew. She knew that Mercy's pupils would be fixed and dilated. She did not want to know, but she knew that her patient with eclampsia had died. Her friend Mercy had died. Ng'etich stopped the compressions. Linda removed the mask. Mercy bent her head slightly backward as if she were trying to take a last breath, but no air moved. Then she was still. Joshua came from behind Linda to his mother's side, and

Linda put her arm around his shoulder. He was too numb to cry yet, but Linda's tears were already washing her face.

But it was an incomplete washing. Ng'etich, who had left to check on his asthma patient, poked his head back in. "I need your help, Linda." She gave Joshua's shoulder a squeeze, said she'd be right back, and followed Ng'etich. As they walked toward the girl with asthma, Ng'etich asked Linda for the rest of the vial of magnesium she had used for Mercy.

"The rest of the vial? Each one was one gram, so I used four vials."

"Really? I thought—" Ng'etich stopped when they got to the room. The girl was tiring. He picked up the box of vials and looked at one with Linda. "It says one gram." He turned the vial slowly. "Per cc. And they are ten cc vials."

Linda gasped. "No. *No!* So I gave her forty grams, not four. That's why her blood pressure and pulse were going down so fast." She clapped her hand over her mouth, and her next words were muffled. "I killed her."

"Linda, let's get some magnesium mixed up for this girl, and…oh! Maybe the vehicle you called Dr. Peel for could bring this girl to the MSF hospital."

Linda didn't move.

Ng'etich touched her arm. "Linda," he said gently. "Could you ask Salome to come and help us get this treatment going?"

Linda's face was expressionless; she walked out and came back with Salome. She watched blankly as Salome and Ng'etich prepared the magnesium. When the MSF vehicle came, she brought the attendant to the asthma patient. Going back to Joshua, she suggested he call his older brother and sister. When the asthma patient left she asked Salome to see if Joshua needed any help. Then she went to where Ng'etich was finishing up, and sat down. He said nothing. She got up, closed the door, and sat down again. "Ng'etich, I killed her. She was my patient, and she was my friend, and I killed her."

Ng'etich sighed, and then furrowed his brow slightly. "Linda, were you angry with Mercy? Did you hate her?"

"What kind of question is that? Of course I didn't hate her. I've known her longer than most anyone else here, and I was very fond of her. I was trying to save her life. I—"

"Then you didn't kill her."

"Ng'etich, I made a mistake mixing up the magnesium. A terrible mistake. She died, not because of eclampsia, but because of the treatment *I* gave her. I killed her!"

"It says in Matthew," Ng'etich said, "that when we are angry with someone, when we call them fools, that kills them. Just like when I want someone who is not my wife, that is adultery. It's what's in my heart that kills people, not what's in my hands. You didn't hate her. You didn't want her to die. That means you didn't kill her."

"Fine…but she's dead, and I caused it."

"Oh yes, she is dead. And maybe mistakes were made. She died—but you can't say you killed her. Killing, stealing, lying, adultery: those are matters of the heart." Linda did not look comforted. "Linda, come to dinner with my wife and me tonight."

*

That evening, Ng'etich answered Linda's *"Hodi"* at the door of his one-bedroom apartment, the left side of one of a cluster of duplexes of staff housing beside the hospital. As she entered the small sitting room, she smelled cooking oil: Ng'etich's wife frying the chapatis that would accompany *dengu* for dinner. Ng'etich parked Linda in an overstuffed chair and left. She scanned the pictures on the walls: the skyline of Paris at night, the American Rocky Mountains in winter, a German castle, an Indonesian beach. Each was the picture from an expired calendar.

After a few minutes, Linda noticed Ng'etich's three-year-old daughter, standing in the doorway between the kitchen and the sitting room, studying Linda. Linda smiled, waved to her, and waited. The girl turned around when her mother, in the kitchen, encouraged her to greet Dr. Linda. After more intense scrutiny, concluding that Dr. Linda was unlikely to eat her, and that her lap looked inviting, the girl approached with her right hand extended. Linda solemnly shook her hand, asked her name, and suggested she climb onto her lap. The girl remained mute, but raised both arms to be picked up. Linda obliged.

Ten minutes later, Ng'etich returned to the sitting room and asked his daughter who her new friend was. The girl pointed at Linda. Ng'etich continued his part of the dialogue verbally; the girl with increasingly animated hand motions and head nods…and smiles. Ng'etich's wife came in and put small tables in front of Linda and Ng'etich, placed a lace doily on each, and returned to the kitchen. She came back with a plate of *dengu* and several chapatis for each of them. Then, still standing, she said, "Let's pray for the food. Dear God, thank you for our guest. Thank you for the food you provide for us. Thank you for life. Amen." She called her daughter and they returned to the kitchen.

"Doesn't your wife eat?" Linda asked Ng'etich.

"Oh sure. She will eat with our daughter in the kitchen."

Linda had almost forgotten why she was there when her cell phone rang. It was Gillian Peel calling. "Hello Gillian… Yes…well, it turns out I'm with Ng'etich now… So I should tell him the girl with asthma is doing well?" She engaged Ng'etich with her eyes; he nodded. "Well, yes, we had planned to send someone with eclampsia. It was Mercy, the woman who worked for me… No…no…no, I'm not OK. Mercy died."

*

On Sunday, Linda went to mass in a funk. She saw Ng'etich walk in ahead of her and move toward the front. She couldn't remember having seen him at mass before. Because she'd never looked? Because this was his first time? She found her usual bench more than halfway back on the left, with the other women. The priest was late, and looked flustered, but then homilized for too long. The microphone malfunctioned, and after a few attempts the priest put it aside and started pacing up and down the center aisle, expostulating. Without the amplified sound, Linda could at least turn him off.

After the homily they sang the creed. And then came the prayers of the faithful. One by one, the children went up to the podium—it was a mass led by children, the priest had announced at the beginning—and said their brief memorized prayers, some in Swahili, some in English. Two or three children disappeared completely behind the podium, even though they were standing on the stool.

Then came the offertory, and the choir began:

*Ni wakati wa sadaka…*
It is the time of offering, but my heart fears
Because I haven't anything to give you, O God.
See all these people offer large gifts;
My lack is that I alone have nothing to offer.

Almost everyone went to the boxes at the front and slipped in a few coins. One small girl in a frilly dress reached up to deposit her shilling in the box, then turned around to find her bench. But the church was big and had many aisles, and she couldn't remember which she had come from. She walked back a bit, faltered, and then stood frozen, looking around. Her eyes began to fill. As the first tear fell from her cheek onto the floor, a woman returning from the collection—a woman she clearly did not know—bent over, said something, and then put her arm around the girl's shoulder and walked her off—but Linda could not see where they went.

The choir continued:

What can I give you, O Lord? I haven't anything to give you;
The offering I have is not pleasing.
My lack is that I alone have nothing to offer.

The people stand with me; they want to give you
Offerings and sacrifices.
My lack is that I alone have nothing to offer.

Putting coins into the boxes wasn't the full offertory, of course; it was a mere collection of money. The ushers carried the boxes to the back, and then lined up to bring them to the altar, led by the altar boys and the dancing girls. First, the adults carried forward the bottle of communion wine and the wafers—which earth had given and human hands had made, and which would shortly be given back to the gathered faithful as the body and blood of their Lord Jesus. Then the boxes of coins, and then the gifts too big to fit in the coin boxes. One woman had a stalk of bananas on her head, another a basket of tomatoes, two men carried a crate of soda, and several adults carried parcels wrapped in newspaper. Three mothers came forward carrying only their infants. All were what the earth had given or human hands had made, and all needed to be consecrated and changed by God, then returned to the faithful, just as the wafers and wine would be.

The choir drove onward:

O Lord, I pray, I have nothing;
Only my heart I give you as my offering.
My lack is that I alone have nothing to offer.

I ask my people: if the Lord has filled you,
Give more so that we all are blessed.
My lack is that I alone have nothing to offer.

O Lord, I pray, bless our work,
The gifts we bring, offerings and sacrifices.
My lack is that I alone have nothing to offer.

After the adults the children followed, carrying their own offerings in the slow procession, herded forward by the ushers. But the procession was too slow for the children in the back, and the line kept bunching, with those in the middle being squeezed. One of them, carrying three small bananas, saw the dancing girls go past and thought that was the best route; she solemnly followed them until an usher scurried out to retrieve her.

These children were very small, none older than preschool, and each carried an offering: a mango, a roll of toilet paper, two tomatoes, a bottle of Fanta, an egg, a bar of soap. As they approached the priest, he took each offering and handed it to the altar boy, who placed it in front of the altar.

A boy not more than four years old walked forward, cradling a large duck egg in both hands, and prepared to hand it to the priest. Just then the line bunched again and he would have been squeezed into the girl in front of him—except that the girl moved to the side just at that moment, and the small boy with the egg was knocked forward and fell, holding the egg to his chest. At first he was stunned. Then he saw that the egg had broken, and the mess covered his new jacket. Turning to the congregation, he wailed his heartbreaking lament.

## Somalia

"Did you ever hear the story of the patient with eclampsia I had that died?" Linda said. It was the day after they'd helped the guard with the stomach ailment, and once more they were sitting outside under the acacia.

"*The* patient?" Mlongo exclaimed. "Seriously, Linda, we've all lost plenty of patients with eclampsia."

"Yes, but this one…well, she was my friend, my houseworker, and I was responsible for her death." And she told Mlongo the story of Mercy.

He listened carefully, and saw right away what Linda was blind to. "So," he played the story back to her, "government hospitals were closed, you and Ng'etich were essentially volunteering, you had almost no support staff, very few drugs, and too many patients. There were no systems in place to double-check for errors, and you all had to do tasks you weren't used to. In the process, Mercy received a toxic dose of magnesium sulfate and died. Now, that is a very long list of factors that led to Mercy's death. And it seems to me that you and the medication error are quite far down that list."

"But if I hadn't given her ten times too much mag sulfate, she might be still alive."

Mlongo smiled—a sad, full smile—and shook his head slightly.

"What is it?" she asked, but he hesitated. "You know," she continued, "we've lived together for a month. We might be killed tomorrow. Go ahead and tell me."

"You *wazungu*," he said. "I've worked with quite a few of you over the years, and *wazungu* seem to think they can do anything. And they usually try, and sometimes they succeed. But if they don't succeed, they're always looking for someone to blame. Usually it's us Kenyans—you know, we didn't try hard enough. But some of the *wazungu* that have been here longer…they know enough not to blame us for everything, so somehow they seem to think it's their fault when things don't work. But why is it anybody's fault?"

Now Linda smiled. "It's funny. Ng'etich wouldn't let me get away with saying I killed Mercy."

"You said you killed Mercy?" Mlongo shook his head slowly. "Sometime I think I understand *wazungu*, but sometimes…" And then he laughed, the first time he had really laughed since they had been captured. A laugh as big as a hug. A laugh she had to join.

"Maybe what the government needs is more Us Guys," Mlongo mused when the laughter had subsided.

"Can *wazungu* be Us Guys?" Linda wondered, swiveling in her plastic chair. Their eyes met. Linda hoped she would have a chance to find out.

# The Doctors Respond

## 1

PROF G WAS ALWAYS on time for one thing: flights. People waited, airplanes didn't. He walked into the departure lounge, which already had half of the two dozen people who were taking the late-afternoon flight to Nairobi. He nodded to two or three he recognized, and as he sat he noticed a white woman with a stethoscope peeking out of her pocket. Could she be the *mzungu* doctor from the District Hospital who Kasamani had mentioned? He walked up and greeted her. "You are Dr. Linda from the District and St. Anthony's, isn't it?"

"Yeeess." Linda nodded. "And you are?"

"Prof G," he said as they shook hands. "I don't think we've formally met, but I used to hear about you when you were at the District."

"You heard about *me?*" Linda asked. "Did I do something wrong?"

"Oh no, quite the opposite. Dr. Kasamani—he was my student, you know—told me about your work. Sometimes I would get referrals from you at the District, and your notes were always quite complete."

Linda smiled. "It's good to hear that someone read them."

"You are surprised?"

"Actually, I am." Linda wasn't sure whether to go on, but Prof G simply waited, his eyes twinkling. "Well, I'm not actually surprised that someone reads the notes as much as that…" Again she hesitated.

Prof G opened the door for her: "It's the care in the District system that bothers you."

"Yes!" Linda continued, relieved. "Well, it did before it closed. There were such shortages when I worked at the District. I mean, it was sometimes hard to get lab or x-rays, especially on the weekends. They ran out of drugs and IV fluids and even syringes and needles. And, of course, nurses: it seems that was the biggest problem. We would sometimes have fifty or sixty kids on the pediatric ward, and only one nurse. And then we'd run out of oxygen or nitrous… And the anesthetists…well, sometimes it was so hard to get them to come." She had been talking faster as she remembered, and her voice started to get strained. She looked up. "I'm sorry—I kind of got carried away."

"No, no, Linda. You are quite right. Things had been getting worse—the same at the Teaching Hospital, until it too closed."

Linda's response was swallowed by the roar of the incoming turboprop plane as it parked on the tarmac outside the waiting area. Just after the left wing-mounted propeller stopped, the door of the plane opened, and the stairs descended. First in line was an old man carrying a walking stick. He rebalanced himself after each successful step down, and when he reached the tarmac he stopped. The passengers behind him began to bunch on the short stairway, until the one directly behind him squeezed around him and shot forward. The old man shuffled a bit, maintaining his central location, and began slowly walking toward the entrance to the terminal. Meanwhile, the other passengers continued to scoot around him, retrieving their bags from the single carousel inside. The old man was the last to enter the terminal.

An announcement then came to board the plane returning to Nairobi, and they walked together to the door, out onto the tarmac, and up the steps of the small plane—Prof climbing stiffly because of his arthritis. There was open seating, and Prof G and Linda sat together. The one flight attendant, wearing a uniform with a skirt that stopped above her knees, closed the door and began the memorized rapid-fire safety instructions: "Ladies and gentlemen, welcome aboard flight number..." followed by the abbreviated "*Mabibi na mabwana, karibuni...*" while the left propeller was restarted.

As they taxied to the runway, Linda tried to recapture the discussion. "You said care was also a problem at the Teaching Hospital? I'm surprised."

"Oh yes. I'm a surgeon, you know. Just before the hospital closed I operated on a one-year-old girl. The operation went very well, and she was awake when she left the theater. We had no complications. But when I came in the next morning, she wasn't there. I don't know what happened—I was just told she had died during the night. Oh yes, we have the same problems you are talking about. And now the patients and families all over Kenya have let us know that something needs to change. In fact, I am on my way to a meeting at the Ministry of Health to discuss this."

"That's good to know. Do you think there might be some changes coming?"

"Of course we are hopeful—but it will be very difficult. You have heard that Ministry allocations to district hospitals have been reduced again?"

"Oh no. Why?"

Prof filled her in on how donors had been cutting back on funding AIDS drugs, and how politically risky it would be to start charging for AIDS care again. So the government decided to pay for the AIDS programs by cutting overall hospital budgets.

Linda sat listening, feeling even more trapped. She wanted to know what the hope was that Prof mentioned, and was just ready to ask when the flight attendant announced that the plane was about to land at Jomo Kenyatta Airport.

Prof said that he would be taking a cab to his hotel; would she like to share a ride? She said she had come to Nairobi "just to get away," and would be glad to share a cab.

Within ten minutes of traveling down the highway toward downtown Nairobi, they were stopped in traffic: what Americans euphemistically called "rush hour" and Kenyans realistically called "jam." *Matatus* bleated on either side, but there was no movement. Their driver laid on his horn for a minute, and then tugged a *Nation* from the dashboard and sat back.

Linda wanted to tap Prof's hope. "OK, Prof. It's very clear; things are getting worse. So how do you keep going? How do you live with this? I mean, I worked in the District Hospital for almost ten years, until I couldn't handle it anymore. So I went back to St. Anthony's. But now it's closed, and…well, another doctor and I are sort of seeing some patients at the District until the government sorts out this problem. But I'm afraid when they reopen St. Anthony's it will be just like before: the patients who need care won't be able to afford it there. So, if the Teaching Hospital is so bad, why do you stay?"

"This is my home. Why do you stay?"

"I sometimes wonder myself."

"No, but you do stay. For what is it, twenty years now, you've stayed. And sure, things may be getting worse. You think it's any easier for us who live here?"

"I guess maybe I did." Linda glanced at Prof, hoping he would tell her it *was* easier, but he said nothing. "OK, I suppose one reason I stay is because I wouldn't fit at home anymore. But that's not really it. When it comes to just treating patients here, I like it. I feel more useful than back home, and the medical practice is more interesting. But even that doesn't get it. Somehow it, I mean everything, seems more…more… well, more *real* here. Am I making sense?"

"So you stay," Prof said after a pause. "And tomorrow I will do what little I can—and it may be nothing—to help us both stay a little longer."

The *matatu* ahead of them inched forward, and the driver laid down his *Nation* and started the engine.

*

The next morning Prof G was at Afya House, waiting outside the office of the Director of Medical Services. Representatives from the Medical Licensing Board and the schools of medicine had been summoned to discuss the district hospital crisis with the DMS, the Deputy DMS, and the Associate Deputy DMS—especially concerning the training of interns. Prof found his colleagues waiting in the outer office of the DMS. Prof Njoroge from the University Council stood to greet Prof G; Dr. Otieno from the Licensing Board, younger, darker, heavier, with more hair, waved from his seat. "You've come back to Nairobi, is it, Prof G?" Njoroge suggested.

"Ah," said Otieno, "he's only here to visit. He was my teacher, you know. And I think our class chased him away, because after he got through with us—or we got through with him, I don't know which—he ran away."

"But I came back to Nairobi—to this office, in fact," Prof G said. "I used to work in this office, you know."

"Yes, and after a couple years, they chased you away, too," Otieno answered.

"But," Njoroge asked, "did you get chased, or did you escape?"

"You know," said Prof G, "without this office, all your graduates would be in private practice."

"Which may be sooner than you think," said Otieno.

The Deputy DMS strode up. "Gentlemen, please come in. The DMS has a bit of an emergency, but we will start our meeting directly." The door of the DMS's office opened only halfway because there was a chair behind it, so the three visitors squeezed in and found seats on a couch and upholstered chairs along the walls of the office.

The DMS, wearing a tailored suit and wire-rimmed glasses, was behind his desk talking with someone on his landline; his desk was clean and polished, but a small table to his left was piled high with booklets, brochures, reports, and calendars. He nodded at the professors as he talked: "Yes…yes…no, no, of course… Another one this morning?… Yes, fifteen more, but are they confirmed?" The conversation went on like this for five minutes. At last he hung up. Placing his hands on the polished wood of the desk, he looked at the seated men. "There has been an outbreak of some hemorrhagic fever in Lodwar," he said. "We know there has been yellow fever in Uganda, so we're assuming it has crossed the border, but of course everyone is worried about Ebola. I think the Associate Deputy DMS can coordinate with the CDC while we proceed. So, thank you gentlemen for coming. Prof G, can I offer you back your chair?" He smiled.

"Oh, but I never occupied that chair, only the one of the Deputy DMS. Except of course when the DMS was away at a meeting."

"Which, if I remember," Njoroge said, "was most of the time." A chuckle rippled around the room.

"So, gentlemen," the DMS said, "let me bring you directly to the point. Some eighty percent of our government hospitals are closed. Community discontent and the nurses' strike seem to be the triggers. We have heard of doctors joining the strikes in sympathy—but not officially. Even some mission and private hospitals are closed due to the strike. MSF proposed setting up field hospitals in Western, Central, and Nyanza…" but here the DMS was interrupted by another call. This one lasted for ten minutes.

Shaking his head, he finally hung up again. "Now, where were we?" he asked.

"The MSF field hospitals," said Otieno.

"Oh yes, yes. So they proposed setting up field hospitals, and we signed agreements with them three weeks ago. The Protestant Health Council is working on a plan to hire unemployed nurses, and several private hospitals have agreed to accept referrals from the MSF and mission hospitals during this crisis, even for patients without insurance, as long as the patient has a true emergency." The DMS looked pleased.

"Now to you: the interns who were in district, provincial, and teaching hospitals are now idle—a workforce of some four hundred doctors—" The DMS's cell phone started singing again. He glanced at the incoming number as he continued talking: "Some four hundred doctors who could be a valuable resource in this crisis. Excuse me, gentlemen." And he answered the call. "Yes, Simon…yes… *Another* one? Oh my God!" Seizing a scrap of paper from the table beside the desk, he started writing while he listened. "Yes, over forty burned…seventeen of those already died… I will ask my deputy to work with you."

The DMS put his phone down and turned to his deputy. "Another tanker has exploded. This one flipped over during the night, and by morning there were hundreds collecting petrol. Then…well, Simon isn't sure what set it off, but the whole thing exploded and is still burning. They have no idea how many were killed, but they've got at least forty with burns—and of course nowhere to take them. Listen, call MSF and ask them to bring in another field hospital now." He looked at his guests, opened his mouth, and then abruptly turned back to the deputy. "Tell MSF to just bring the supplies now. We'll provide the doctors." And the Deputy DMS hurried out.

The DMS shook his head slightly, closed his eyes, and then opened them. "My proposal, gentlemen, is that we redeploy the interns that are now idle. There are consultants in some of the larger private and mission hospitals, and the interns could be a valuable help to them."

"But do we have enough to supervise nearly four hundred interns?" Otieno asked.

"No, not in the private system. But we have plenty of consultants in the Ministry and in the teaching hospitals…"

"…who are now on strike," Njoroge reminded him.

"Ah, that is the point," the DMS said. "*They* are not actually on strike, the *nurses* are. An illegal strike, by the way. But that is another matter. We are considering redeploying the consultants as well—to where the interns are sent, and to the MSF field hospitals that are being set up. Which means we could send interns to those field hospitals. So these are our proposals, but they are just that: proposals. So, Dr. Otieno, how would the Licensing Board view this sort of arrangement? Would you consider this an acceptable experience for the interns to be fully licensed when they finish?"

The ensuing discussion was, if not lively, certainly heartfelt. Or appeared to be heartfelt. Everyone spoke with passion and conviction, clearly articulating the dangers as well as the benefits of the DMS plan for interns. At the end, the DMS was assured of the full support of the professors and the board for the plan he outlined for interns.

And then Prof G said, "Bwana DMS, may I raise an AOB?"

"Any Other Business is most welcome," the DMS proclaimed, and added quietly, "as long as we can handle it in thirty seconds"—to the grins of his guests.

"Fine," Prof G said. "I'll be brief. So, we've approved your current crisis mode management for interns. What's next?"

The DMS said nothing at first, expecting a far lengthier AOB. Then: "You mean what's next in our meeting? What disaster will we confront next?"

"A bit beyond that. How do you think we can get these district hospitals opened up again—how, and how soon?"

The DMS smiled, a bit grimly. "You know, it seems to me the people have spoken, Prof. They don't want our hospitals, and apparently neither do the nurses. And the IMF says we spend too much money on free services. Maybe we need to listen to them; maybe they are right."

"Meaning...?"

"Look at the facts, Prof. Doctors are leaving the Ministry faster than we can replace them with new graduates. And where do they go? To the NGOs and the private hospitals, where they make more money than we can pay them. So, what is the future of the district hospitals if neither the doctors, nor the nurses, nor even the patients, appreciate them?"

"Fine," Prof said, but the twinkle had left his eyes.

**2**

The four-wheel-drive pickup with the huge antenna sticking up from the front bumper and "MSF" emblazoned on the door sped into the compound, followed by a cloud of dust that engulfed the vehicle when it stopped. Gillian Peel jumped down from the back holding an infant with one arm and an IV bag with the other. An old woman clambered nimbly down after Gillian and followed her into a huge canvas tent. "I got a dry one," Gillian barked as she rushed in. "I need another bag of saline. And bring the amp and gent—I'll bet this kid's septic." She immediately found a nurse and the doctor on call at her side. "This is the granny," she informed them, tipping her head toward the old woman. "The mum's away at teachers college."

"Kid's pretty skinny too," said Roger, the other doctor.

"Sick as shit," said Gillian, "but I think we can pull this one through. Soon as the diarrhea stops and the kid's hydrated again, she'll need the feeding unit. Is it set up yet, Hu?"

"We had the first three admissions today," Hu Nguyen, the nurse, answered. "By the looks of things, the unit will be full before the week is finished."

"Then we'll double the size. Bloody hell, all these kids need is food. Food! That's not rocket science."

Gillian left the tent and headed for the administration office. MSF had been allotted the facilities of a remote health center, forty-five minutes away from St. Anthony's and the District Hospital. The health center had been upgraded to a hospital a year previously, but construction for the expansion had stalled. Now MSF had been assigned to four upgraded health centers throughout the country; health centers they could rapidly equip as hospitals—and leave the buildings when they left. All parties saw this as a form of capacity building.

MSF erected the huge white tent as a temporary admission and stabilization unit while they completed the construction of the wards and operating theater. Gillian, with her seniority at MSF, had been chosen as hospital director for this site, and she immediately offered employment to the existing staff at the center; all readily agreed, as MSF would be topping up their salary. They had been open for three weeks now. As soon as their theater was finished, Dr. Kasamani would be coming as their surgeon. And with him, four interns.

The administration office was in a separate building that contained the outpatient examining rooms, the lab, and the pharmacy—the original health center, in fact. Gillian found a long line of people waiting, and stopped in first at the examining room to find out if the clinical officer needed help. He was sitting at his desk, reading the *Standard*. "Excuse me, Simiyu, but there is a long line of patients waiting. Is this the best time to read the newspaper?"

"Oh no, Daktari, I have checked severally. Those people are waiting to see you."

"Simiyu, I told you that all patients must be screened by clinical officers first. People see an *mzungu* and they think we can walk on water. We can't."

"No, Daktari, they are not patients. They came to see the director."

"What for?"

"I don't know. They didn't say."

The first two people she talked with were looking for jobs. Two, she decided, was a pattern, so she stood outside her office and made a general announcement that she appreciated everyone's interest in the new hospital, but that there were no job openings at present. She assured them that if jobs became available, she would notify the district commissioner at the same time as the adverts went in the newspaper.

Several people left. She called the next one in, a barefoot woman in her sixties, wearing a torn dress. "How can I help you?" Gillian asked.

"*Si sikii kizungu,*" the woman responded.

"Great," Gillian mumbled. She got up, looking around, and found Simiyu. "Hey, do you know anyone who can translate for me?"

"Sure," he said. "I'm not doing anything." And they went in together. Simiyu greeted the woman, who then began a lengthy conversation. Knowing there were several others waiting, Gillian interrupted them and asked Simiyu what the woman wanted. "Oh, I don't know," he answered. "She was telling me where she was from and that she had known my mother many years ago. She comes from down here." He pointed out the window. "Past where the river goes next to the road—you know the place? You pass it when you take the road that comes in here. That was my mother's home…"

"Come on, Simiyu. There's a long line. Ask her what she wants." There followed another lengthy exchange, and after five minutes she broke in. "Well?"

"She is telling me she is grateful that you have agreed to see her."

"Fine. What does she want?"

More exchanges that showed no sign of abating.

"Simiyu, what is all this? What does she want?"

"She says she wants a job."

"Tell her—"

"Actually I am telling her that you've been a very good hospital director, and that you would like to give her a job—"

"We have no jobs!"

"—but that as of today there are no openings, though there might be some openings tomorrow."

"But Simiyu, why build up false hopes?"

"Yes, but Daktari, it is not good to crush hope."

By late afternoon, when Gillian had finished saying no to all those who wanted jobs, she dropped by the big treatment tent again. The infant she had brought in was already looking better. Dr. Roger Laducier, her Canadian colleague, had given the first dose of antibiotics to the baby, and Hu was showing the mother how to use oral rehydration.

"How's the ward?" Gillian asked.

"Pretty quiet now," Roger answered. "The fellow with AIDS and PCP pneumonia finally died."

"Did you get the sputum tested for TB?"

"It was negative—but we had him isolated anyway."

"Enjoy the quiet. When theater opens things will be sort of crazy here."

The three walked back together to their tents. The health center had only two small houses, already occupied when MSF arrived, so Gillian had set up temporary quarters for the expats just beyond the two houses. She also reinforced the fence around the compound, hired an extra guard, and built another fence around their living space. An old, unused mud-and-wattle hut with a rusty iron roof became their kitchen. On either side, in two rows facing each other, she set up half a dozen tents: one each for sleeping, one for a common space, and the other two for storage. Between them was a large shade tree. At the other end were the pit latrines and bathing place. There was electricity in the clinical areas, but it had not yet been installed in the living areas; they had solar panels and batteries for their lights, music, and computers. Standard relief-worker fare.

Gillian brought out three chairs and set them up under the tree; Roger went to the kitchen hut and brought back three Tuskers. Hu removed the caps and passed them around. Gillian sat, exhaled deeply, and closed her eyes as a thin breeze brushed her face. "So, Gil," Roger said after two swallows, "how come you keep coming back to Kenya?"

"Meaning?"

"Well, you did Somalia back when that was still possible, you've done Congo—so why Kenya?"

"Shit, Rog, you sound like Mlongo. It's not about war, it's about people who need help."

Hu joined: "People here sure need help. We had another malnourished kid come in today—after the one you brought. I was at public health the other day and checked their stats. They said five percent malnutrition. That's *severe* malnutrition—about the same as we saw in some places in Sudan."

"Well, but I saw a guy the other day with diabetes. Type two," said Roger. "He wasn't fat, but he wasn't skinny either. So what's going on?"

"Too much of the wrong kind of food for some people," said Hu. "Not enough of the right kind for the kids I see. But why? It's green here year round. How come there are malnourished kids here?"

No one answered. They watched as a rooster chased a hen around their compound. "So listen," Gillian said after a pause. "Enjoy the quiet, maybe two more weeks. I'm going to push for the theater to get finished, and when Kasamani comes we're going to be packed. There's no government facilities around here working, so there's surely a backlog. We've got an MSF anesthetist coming for the first two months the theater is open, then the Ministry says they'll send one."

"Space?" Roger asked.

"We've got the plans for a couple of wards—done in six months max. I've got another tent coming. Listen, as long as the patients are here, I'll make sure you've got what you need."

## 3

The AIDS Institute, too, was determined to be in the forefront of responses to Kenya's health care needs. Four of the key players met at the new Chinese-French restaurant at the edge of town that evening. "Chinese-French?" Dr. Hodges had asked after Mlongo suggested they try it. "Is it Chinese or French?"

"It is actually both," Mlongo explained. "Haven't you heard of fusion restaurants? You can get Chinese dishes and French dishes."

Hodges grinned. "But the waiters: are they Chinese or French? I mean, at home the defining characteristic of most Chinese restaurants is the Chinese waiters."

"The waiters are Kenyan, Dr. Hodges."

Hellen, KK, Mlongo, and Hodges (graciously holding the door open for all of them) filed into the restaurant. The decor was distinctly upscale: low lights with candles on the tables, tablecloths, cloth napkins folded into cones, a uniformed waiter guiding them to a quiet table in the corner by a window, and across the room several other uniformed waiters hovering near the bar with their backs to the large television on which was a British soccer match. One of them was immediately at their table with menus, taking their orders for drinks.

"These dishes look very interesting," Mlongo finally said.

"You can read Chinese?" Hellen asked. The menus contained Chinese characters transliterated into English, but still giving no clue about what the dish was.

"Oh no," he said, "I'm on the French page."

"And the little blurb under each tells what's in it,"

KK said, "like mushrooms or steak or mixed vegetables or whatever. But I can't find what I want."

"What's that, KK?" Hodges asked.

"Chicken and *ugali* with *sukuma wiki*."

Hellen started laughing. "KK, you probably have that every time you eat out. You don't want some of this *moo goo gai pan?* Or green peppers with bamboo shoots, or sweet-and-sour pork?"

"How can it be sweet and sour at the same time?" KK wondered.

Mlongo smiled. "Or how about this *coquille St. Jacques gratinées?* Or maybe quiche lorraine, or *soufflé au fromage?*"

"Oh yes," said KK quickly, "you want me to get outside my comfort envelope—isn't that what the Americans call it?" addressing Hodges.

Hodges pretended to stroke the chin that wasn't there. "We get outside the comfort *zone,* KK. I believe you might be referring to *pushing* the envelope. Which, as a concept, actually overlaps with the 'zone' concept," he said in mock seriousness.

"Oh, yes, yes," said KK, "that fits very well. The envelope is a mathematical or aeronautical concept within which one is quite safe, but when the boundaries of that safe envelope are exceeded, the risk correspondingly increases. So of course one is no longer comfortable."

Hodges kept stroking as KK talked. Mlongo looked

at him, nodding seriously, but Hellen erupted in laughter.

"So, KK," she said between giggles, "does this idea get written down on your index cards? And could we use it as our conceptual framework in one of our studies?"

"Yes, yes, I suppose I could write it down," he said, pulling out his cards, "but which study do you think we could use it for?" By now they were all laughing—KK with them, though he wasn't entirely sure of the joke.

"Well, first," said Hellen, "we could use it as a conceptual framework for this meal. Will you be pushing the envelope with this meal?" she asked KK.

"If I have to," he said, "because I can't find chicken and *ugali* with *sukuma wiki* on the menu."

Mlongo rescued him, smiling. "KK, the owner is a friend of mine. No worries. I can assure you that you will not be the first to come into the restaurant with that order—let me say I know this from personal experience."

"In other words, that's what you usually get here?" Hellen asked.

"No, not *usually*. But, yes, I have been known to eat chicken and *ugali* here."

They all ordered—with KK being assured that even though chicken, *ugali,* and *sukuma* were not on the menu, he would be served them—and then Hodges outlined why he had invited them all to dinner.

"Now, Leonard and I have been having some pretty intense discussions about the events of the last month or so—in fact, it was when you stopped in a couple weeks ago, Hellen, that we really began to focus on some of the key issues—and we agreed that we in the AIDS Institute are at a critical juncture. It is precisely your expertise in research"—he nodded at KK—"and your overall epidemiological view"—nodding at Hellen—"that prompted us to convene this little get-together. And as you both represent the university, we felt it was time to make our relationship even more explicit."

Hellen and KK waited.

"Well then," Hodges continued, "let me get right to the point. Data coming in from the NMPSP—and I just got the latest report from Geneva yesterday—are compelling: the prevalence of some of the chronic conditions and risk factors we've been screening for is far higher than any of us imagined. And that means the epidemiological transition is far more advanced than we thought. Leonard, would you like to pick up from here?"

"Yes, well, my former director here"—indicating Hodges—"and I are pretty much in agreement that as we have over the last decade rather vigorously confronted AIDS, we need to do the same with many other chronic diseases, and—"

"Leonard, I asked you to pick up the thread here

precisely because we are *not* in complete agreement on some points. I don't want to represent your position inaccurately. Let's get everything on the table, and then we can see what sort of studies can move us ahead, together with our university colleagues here."

"Well…" As Mlongo was gathering his thoughts, the waiter came with four colossal white porcelain plates, releasing a fusion of smells: grilled chicken, baked cheese, sweet-and-sour sauce, and scallops. Even the *ugali* and *sukuma* looked elegant. When everyone was served, Mlongo continued. "I think what my former director is referring to here is what you might call the two sides of primary care: the acute conditions we have always treated, and the emerging conditions that are presenting themselves so forcefully in these NMPSP statistics. They are both there: on that we agree. The point of difference, if we have one, is which of these two we—especially we at the Institutes—should be focusing on. Is that what you were referring to, Dr. Hodges?"

"Exactly." Hodges sliced off a neat corner of quiche and held it suspended halfway to his mouth. "Except that I might even put a sharper point on it. My argument is that compelling evidence coming out of NMPSP points to the need for a different model of health services countrywide, one that prepares us for the onslaught of these chronic diseases that are coming. Well, not just coming; they are already here. KK and Hellen, we've laid out the issue; what do you folks think?"

KK was ripping intently at his chicken, so Hellen put down her knife and fork and turned to Hodges. "Now, Alan, I want to make sure I understand. What you seem to be saying is that the way the US was a hundred years ago is the way we are now—things like health services, burden of disease, and the like." Hodges listened, but was careful about assenting until Hellen finished. "And, further, you seem to be implying that the way the US is now is a sort of picture of what we will be like in the future. Did I get you correctly?"

"That is, of course, a gross oversimplification of the epidemiological transition—but yes, there is some truth in that capsule summary. I'm saying Kenya should not need to reinvent the wheel. I'm saying if there are some lessons we Americans learned the hard way, wouldn't it make sense for Kenyans to use them as a starting point? To adapt them, of course, but to at least start with them."

"OK, sure," Hellen answered. "But to take you back just a bit: how do we know that Kenyan disease patterns will develop along the same lines as America? Surely there are some major differences in our history and economy—and certainly our climate—compared with yours. Are we bound to repeat your history?"

"That's exactly my point, Hellen. We hope you will *not* repeat our history. It took us far too long to develop a system to confront chronic disease. We want to save you from those mistakes we made."

"No, Alan, I mean your history of *burden* of disease. Are we bound to undergo the same changes you did—moving from the infectious diseases of poverty to the degenerative diseases of industrialization?"

"Oh, but Hellen, it's not just the US! This is a pattern internationally, demonstrated time and time again. It's a matter of history. That's just what happens. You can deny history, or you can learn from it. I'd prefer to learn from it, wouldn't you?"

"But isn't it possible to break free of it, at least a bit? I mean, is there something inherent in human nature that a people have to die of heart disease once they've conquered pneumonia and diarrhea? If we had so little heart disease only ten years ago, *must* we get it, the way you and the Europeans have?"

Hodges, caught off guard by this line of reasoning, was considering his response, but KK had finished his chicken, and was ready to engage. "Excuse me, Dr. Hodges, but let's go back—back to before the food came. You said you had got the latest stats from Geneva, and that chronic disease rates are very high in Kenya. Of course that refers to the households that accepted screening, because we have no data from those who refused."

"Yes, of course."

"I assume you know that over fifty percent of households refused screening."

"I knew there was a certain percent, but I wasn't aware of the exact figure."

"Yes, yes. Fifty-six percent. Now, early on when Hellen and I were looking at these numbers, we found that rural people were generally pretty open to being screened, and that town people were suspicious. Well, since we've had these hospital closures, refusals among rural people have been very high—in some places over ninety percent. So now the people who are accepting screening are the people less affected by the government closures, people in perhaps a higher economic class, people more at risk for these chronic diseases. So yes, we have higher rates than we expected of chronic diseases…*among some people.*" KK paused, and then went on more slowly. "But we just don't know about the rest."

"And what we do know, from other studies," Hellen added, "is that those who do use—or I should say used to use—government hospitals have the pattern of acute infectious diseases we are all well aware of."

Mlongo, having had a chance to work on his *coquille St. Jacques gratinées*, was now ready to come back in. "What I'm hearing from all of us is, I think, exactly the point Dr. Hodges was asking me to outline: that there are two realities here, and which one you look at will determine how you act. So we have two disease patterns in Kenya. Kenya is not either one or the other; it's both."

"Like sweet-and-sour pork?" KK asked. Everyone

stared at him for just a moment, and then Hodges covered his small chin with the palm of his left hand. "Yes, KK," he said, extending his right index finger. "Yes. And speaking of which, would anyone like this *omelette à la Norvégienne* for dessert?"

"I'm not sure about an omelet for dessert," Hellen said.

"Oh no," said Hodges, "this is what we in the States call baked Alaska: it has ice cream in the middle, surrounded by cake and then meringue, which of course need to be baked. So it is both hot and cold—at the same time."

Hellen was now suppressing a laugh. "I'll try it." The laugh bubbled up. "This looks like something you need to put on your index cards, KK."

"Well, I could, but I think I need to sample it first."

They ordered four servings, and while they were waiting, Hodges returned to the earlier topic. "Do we have two *realities,* or two *populations?* There is only one *reality,* isn't there, Leonard? And we describe it, albeit imperfectly"—nodding to KK—"by the statistics emanating from our studies. So of course we refine our studies to better describe the reality that is here. I mean, some things are plain and simple facts." Hodges looked up toward the door, and returned to the conversation with a metaphor. "For example," he said, "we can argue about interpretation, but not about facts. So, whether you like them or not, three policemen just walked into the restaurant."

Mlongo, opposite him with his back to the door, froze. "Oh no," he said quietly. "I think it's best if you don't get up right now—and *don't even look at them. And Dr. Hodges, please don't argue with them and do exactly what they say.*"

Three more men with police uniforms and assault rifles came in. The restaurant had fallen silent. Two of the men went into the kitchen, and the four who remained distributed themselves around the restaurant and started barking commands.

"Everyone get down on the floor and lie there. *Chini kabisa.* Don't look up. Now, all cell phones and wallets—all of them, *sasa hivi.* All the money you've got. Car keys too. *Now!*"

There was scraping of chairs and rustling as the customers dropped to the floor, and someone whimpered.

"Shut up!" the man closest to the door said. "Now, now! All your phones, money, and keys. *Pesa zote.*" The "police" walked around picking up keys, phones, and wallets, removing the money, and tossing the wallets back on the floor. One went out to the parking lot, and they heard a car engine start. Through the legs of the chairs and tables, Hodges saw a man lift his head. Immediately, a police boot slammed into his temple and he groaned. "No looking or we kill you!"

Within five minutes the thieves had left, and they heard a car disappear into the night. But it was another minute or two before anyone dared to look up. At first Mlongo heard muffled protests, and when they were not met by more police boots, he crept over to the man who had been kicked. A raw wound oozed on the side of his face, but there was no active bleeding and he was awake and alert. By then, the protests had turned to impotent outrage. One of the waiters peered out the door, and finding no more gangsters, went out to discover the guard tied up, and car keys scattered on the gravel. He freed the guard and brought the keys back in, and the customers who had retrieved their empty wallets pawed through the pile of keys on the head waiter's desk, hoping theirs wasn't the car the thieves had left in.

A few of those who found their keys left immediately, without paying. As the others milled around, the head waiter announced that he was very sorry, that their security firm was sending several extra guards immediately, and that everyone was invited for a drink on the house. Mlongo looked at his colleagues. Hellen said she still wanted that hot-and-cold dessert. KK nodded, and Hodges, swallowing hard, said he would go along with the group. Mlongo ordered a carafe of white wine.

But Hodges was jumpy. "So what happens now? Are the police on the way? Will there be some sort of investigation? Will we need to give statements?"

Mlongo looked around the table. Hellen, seeing no other takers, took the question. "Yes, Alan, the police will probably come—maybe after a while. They'd get here quicker if the restaurant owner sends a vehicle to pick them up—but he'll probably wait for them."

"But there are undoubtedly clues they can find; fingerprints or something. I mean, can't they interview the shop owners nearby to see if anyone saw anything? Surely they can't have gotten very far…"

"Actually, Dr. Hodges," Mlongo said, "I think the police know this group of gangsters very well. In fact, so does anyone who reads the newspapers—they've been hitting different restaurants around town every week or two. Same style."

"Well then, surely the police have some clues, some sort of plan…"

"Oh yes," said KK. "Where do you think these guys got those police uniforms?"

Hodges was not familiar with dead ends. "OK, then what about the police chief, or maybe the regional police chief? Has anybody taken this thing higher up?" His three tablemates looked at each other. "I mean, it sounds like, well, if the police are part of this, shouldn't that be reported? You guys must know who could do something about this…don't you?"

Mlongo opened his mouth, then looked down at the table and shook his head slightly.

"So you mean no one is going to do anything?" Hodges said.

"Oh, these guys will die," Hellen said offhandedly.

"What do you mean?" Hodges asked.

"Someone will kill them. They'll get greedy, or make a mistake, or misjudge something, and someone will kill them."

"Who?"

"Army, GSU, I don't know. Maybe just a crowd of people."

"But wouldn't it be better to arrest them and bring them to justice?"

"Justice?" KK asked. "In Kenyan courts?"

They did not have to pursue this; their *omelette à la Norvégienne* came, and they all were appropriately impressed how it could be both hot and cold at the same time.

Hodges cut through the meringue crust with his spoon. "Hot and cold. Sweet and sour. Acute and chronic diseases: both at the same time. That's what we were talking about when we were so rudely interrupted." He gave a grim smile. "That we have these two populations in Kenya, and that our health system needs to cater to both. Or at least that is my contention—and I am proposing that we address this issue in an academic fashion." He took a bite. "But it sounds like the first thing we need is accurate statistics, especially taking into consideration those who have refused screening."

"We're with you there, Alan," said Hellen. "KK and I will have something for you, oh, in about two days. How do you see it, KK?"

"Exactly."

## 4

Nothing, in a crisis, is permanent. In just a month, Gillian's MSF project moved to the District Hospital as part of another unique public–private partnership: the Ministry was using medical NGOs to reopen district hospitals and "rehabilitate" them during the coming year. Linda returned there, Ng'etich remained, and Kasamani had come back. He still operated at St. Anthony's as well, which had reopened long before MSF arrived at the District. Both hospitals were busy, and the NMPSP project remained active, sending newly discovered diabetics and hypertensives to chronic disease clinics at both places, overseen by the newly expanded AIDS Institute—now truly a Chronic Disease Institute. Each hospital gradually found a niche: St. Anthony's expanded chronic disease care and elective surgery, and the District again became the focus for acute care and most of the trauma. St. Anthony's developed a hospice, and the District expanded their pediatric ward.

When Gillian first came to the District, she was glad to have the experienced staff there, and was impressed by the careful work Linda and Ng'etich had managed to maintain—in a District Hospital that wasn't even open. But by her second week there, she noticed marked but subtle resistance by the nurses to the routine use of magnesium sulfate for women with eclampsia. She mentioned this in passing one day to

Linda, and Linda suddenly looked wretched. But only for a moment: she quickly recovered and offered to give Gillian some "background."

They walked to Gillian's office: standard government-issue furniture, but with a large poster on the wall advertising a music festival in Iceland, proceeds going to MSF. Linda told Gillian the whole story of Mercy's death; told her in some detail the story that she would never forget, but that she had never talked about—and hadn't yet opened again with Ng'etich and Salome. She told Gillian that she understood the hesitation by some nurses to use a drug that obviously had a reputation for being dangerous.

Gillian listened carefully, reminded of the times she too had inadvertently participated in the death of a patient. Now, as administrator, her concern was more immediate. "Do you mean," she asked, "that we'll never be able to use mag sulfate here?"

"Not at all. I mean that it will take some time. Tell you what: let me work on maternity for the next couple weeks, and help set up the mag sulfate protocol there."

"Are you sure that's OK for you?"

"No," Linda admitted, "I'm not sure. But I'm ready to find out."

*

Two weeks later, Gillian asked Linda if she could pick her brain again.

"Sure," Linda said, and they went back to Gillian's office. "What's going on?"

"Well, first, just an FYI: the maternity nurses just reordered magnesium sulfate."

Linda smiled and nodded.

"So, um…good work." Gillian got up, closed the office door, and sat down again. Then she started her story. She told Linda that when she went back to work with MSF, she hadn't really finished her work with NMPSP in the refugee camps. Things were on hold for a while, but there, as here, the screening was picking up again. Distances were great, and the people were pastoralists, so any kind of screening was difficult. But she did notice, as she saw here at St. Anthony's and the District, that the NMPSP money seemed to have a positive effect on the clinical services themselves. "So," she asked Linda, "is this effect real? Can you really give better care because of all this money?"

"Oh, it's real enough now," Linda affirmed. "I'm just not sure how…" She trailed off, looking out the window.

"…how sustainable it is," Gillian finished.

Linda was silent for a moment, then turned back to face Gillian. "Yeah, but also how many people can actually make use of these services, even now. When I was at St. Anthony's this last time, I was too busy to do any financial screening, but I know what happened ten years ago: people stopped going there because they couldn't afford the place. I wonder how many are just choosing not to go there now, and come here instead."

"But didn't the District sort of benefit from money coming in through NMPSP?"

"It was *supposed* to. But the protests about poor care and the closures came *after* NMPSP started. I suspect the District didn't benefit as much from NMPSP as St. Anthony's did."

"In all the projects I've worked on, especially in relief," Gillian reflected, "patient finances have never come into it. The organization pays for everything." They both sat quietly for a minute. "Anyway, I'm planning to get back up to Northeastern to see some of the screening in the Dadaab camps themselves, and also what's happening with the teams we send out to screen the pastoralists. I went out several times before I came down here; it's quite interesting. You ought to come up sometime and see what we do. In fact, I'm going on a trip next week. Len Mlongo will be going too. Why don't you join us?"

"A month or two ago I would have said yes, but it's gotten pretty busy lately, and I don't see any letup soon. Thanks, though."

Again Gillian sat quietly, and Linda waited. "Um… there's something else," Gillian said finally, and she told Linda the story of her Pap smears, with the news she had received earlier in the week: the latest follow-up smear had been strongly positive, and she was going to have directed biopsies. "I'm assuming they'll be OK— at least, Len says the first procedure usually takes care of everything. But if they confirm the cancer returned, it looks like a hysterectomy." Linda reached across and grasped both of Gillian's hands with her own, squeezed lightly, and said nothing. Gillian realized why she had chosen to tell her story to this person she hardly knew.

## Somalia

For the last two weeks, Mlongo and Linda had allowed themselves to relax a bit. They had routines, they knew their guards, and—since the diarrhea incident with the tall one—the guards allowed themselves some small talk with their captives.

Several days after taking the herbs and homemade ORS, the tall guard was on duty alone. From across the compound he said a few sentences to Mlongo, then proclaimed in English, "Strong," and he bent his right elbow and made a fist.

Linda looked at Mlongo. "What's going on? More trouble?"

Mlongo grinned. "I'm sure there will be, but just now the guard was telling me how strong he feels after our superb medical intervention."

"ORS sure is effective," Linda said.

Mlongo noticed the twinkle in her eye, and added, "Together with herbs."

And the guard again said, "Strong," elbow bent, fist shaking, and this time he smiled.

Then one day several more keffiyeh-wearing men with AK-47s showed up, and Mlongo's and Linda's fear during the first week flooded back. The next day they were told to get into the back of an open lorry, and again they were handcuffed together at the ankles. The ride was bumpy, windy, dusty, and hot, and the sides of the lorry were high enough to keep them from seeing any of the landscape. After some twenty minutes the lorry stopped, and they were pushed out and into the back room of a mud-and-wattle dwelling with an iron roof, each now with their own ankle cuffs.

The room was divided by a curtain. Linda was shoved into one side, Mlongo the other. On Linda's side there was a single window, closed by a wooden shutter; the room was dark except for the light coming from the front room. She could not see outside; she saw only the back of her guard, who had a chain tied around his waist that was linked to her ankle cuffs. A second guard had the chain from Mlongo's cuffs wrapped around his waist. These were the same two teenage boys who had greeted her and Mlongo with AK-47 assault rifles in the Dadaab refugee camp a month earlier.

"Mlongo," Linda said to the curtain. Her guard turned, looked at her, scowled, then returned to his conversation.

"Yes, Linda."

"How are you doing?"

"I'm here."

Dusk came, but no food, no mattresses. One guard lit the lantern, but the other snapped at him, and he put it out. The lorry that had brought them had driven off, and they saw only the two guards. Mlongo and Linda knew that this was not a time to talk.

Hours passed. Linda leaned back against the wall and drifted. She became aware of a Somali conversation in the front room, then drifted again. She heard Mlongo breathe like he was sleeping— she had come to know the sound well—and then it stopped. He was awake again. She felt like she had the first night they had been kidnapped, only worse. The guards now weren't jubilant; they were jumpy.

# The Boy with the
# Broken Egg

## 1

It was mid-December, and Hellen was doing Christmas shopping at the downtown Nakumatt. At the front entrance, a plastic Santa Claus danced a mechanical jig to "Rudolph the Red-Nosed Reindeer," and artificial snow was sprayed on the front windows. Hellen had walked from home, and she was hot when she arrived. In the flour aisle, she found Prof G. He turned when Hellen greeted him.

"Good morning. I am buying millet flour," he announced.

"Millet flour," Hellen acknowledged. "I see that. You are preparing for holiday *uji*?"

"Yes, but not just holiday *uji*. Any day *uji*. We cannot grow millet in town, so I must buy the flour here. Are you buying millet for Christmas *uji*?"

"Ah, no. My daughter is coming in from Nairobi, so I'm buying cornflakes."

"Well, of course," Prof G said, "I am also buying cornflakes. By the way, have you heard anything about those kidnappings in Dadaab? It sounds like they were people involved with NMPSP."

"Yes, I heard something about that. I assumed they were some of the screeners going house to house. Why? What have you heard?"

"Well, news reports said that some were international health workers. I wonder if it's any of the people working through the AIDS Institute."

"I hadn't stopped to think—but of course they would kidnap expats. They wouldn't get much money out of Kenyans. Do you know who they are?"

"There were no names in the *Nation*; I haven't seen the *Standard* yet. I wonder if it's that young British doctor Mlongo engaged to work up there."

"Oh yes, I met her several times with Mlongo. Her name was Peel—Gillian, I think. She seemed like the type who liked to go to dangerous places. And to speak her mind."

Prof G opened his eyes wider.

"Yes," Hellen continued, "the type who might be kidnapped. I'll stop by the Institute on the way home—maybe Mlongo knows something."

"Let me call Kasamani first," Prof said. "He's been pretty involved out there at the District and with St. Anthony's; maybe he knows something."

He called—but other than noting the news report, Kasamani had nothing to add. Gillian Peel had been around until last week, and had mentioned something about an upcoming trip to Dadaab… No, Dr. Jankowski was away for the holidays.

When Hellen left Nakumatt, she dropped in at the Institute, but found it closed for the holidays. She tried Mlongo's cell number, but an efficient British voice told her, "The mobile phone you are trying to reach has been switched off." She walked home, still wondering which health workers had been kidnapped, and whether or not this would become a pattern, a new source of income for pirates.

## 2

Two days before Christmas, Prof G was visited at his home by a small, middle-aged gentleman with a trim mustache representing, his card said, the EA Security Company. Prof G kindly but directly informed him that this was his home, he was on holiday, and he preferred to take care of business at the office. The gentleman responded equally kindly and directly that this was not a routine business call, that he had been engaged by the AIDS Institute to investigate a kidnapping likely involving at least one employee of the Institute, and perhaps others, and that he was led to believe that Prof G might be able to give him some background information. Prof G granted that, having read about the kidnapping in the newspapers, he possibly knew some of those who had been kidnapped. He invited the gentleman, who now introduced himself as Mr. Muranga, to have a seat.

Prof G's sitting room had two couches, four stuffed chairs, and several straight-backed wooden chairs. Mr. Muranga sat at the end of one of the couches, and Prof G sat opposite him. Prof G's wife brought in a thermos of tea and a plate of biscuits.

Mr. Muranga proceeded, at Prof's request, to outline the events as he knew them. Over a week ago, the Kenya police in one of the Dadaab refugee camps had been informed that some health workers who had been involved with surveys were missing. The surveys were being done by the NMPSP, and those missing were apparently supervisors who had come to evaluate the program. The next day Al Shabaab took responsibility for the kidnapping, saying it was holding two hostages, one a Kenyan and one a foreigner. Did the professor have an idea who they might be?

Prof G responded that Dr. Leonard Mlongo, the director of the AIDS Institute, was deeply involved in the NMPSP, including some screening efforts in refugee areas.

"Interesting," Mr. Muranga said. "I was just in Dadaab, finding out what I could. At the UN compound I spoke with the bartender from the Pumzika Club. He said he had been told the man kidnapped was one of his customers. In fact, he remembered bringing chicken and chips to a table with several people who apparently didn't know each other and were just getting acquainted, and the man who would eventually be kidnapped was among them. As the bartender was leaving the table, he heard one of the people at the table say to the man and a white woman, 'Oh, so you work together.' We have reason to believe the man may have been Leonard Mlongo. Do you know who the woman might have been?"

"Yes," said Prof G. "Dr. Mlongo's close associate in the work in Dadaab was a Dr. Gillian Peel. He had recruited her to work in that area because she had extensive experience in refugee and relief work."

"And her nationality?"

"British."

"Thank you, Professor. I will contact the British embassy. Do you have a contact for Dr. Peel?"

"I can find one," he said, and called Hellen. He gave a number to Mr. Muranga, who tried it, but the phone had been turned off. "Yes, it looks like you had better contact the British Embassy," Prof G said. "Please let me know what you find."

3

Several hours later, Prof G received a call from Mr. Muranga, who said that his ongoing efforts on behalf of the AIDS Institute were bearing interesting but un-expected fruit. He'd discovered that a Dr. Gillian Peel was a patient in the Nairobi Hospital. Could Prof G be of any assistance in finding out if this was the same

Dr. Gillian Peel he had previously referred to and, if so, why she was in the Nairobi Hospital? Prof G said he would make some phone calls and get back to Mr. Muranga.

As his first thought was trauma, he contacted a surgical colleague at Nairobi Hospital. The colleague had no such patient, but was in the hospital and offered to check the admission list. Five minutes later he called back: Gillian Peel had been admitted a few days ago and was recovering from a hysterectomy. Prof G called Mr. Muranga and told him that Dr. Gillian Peel was not the second person kidnapped. "Then," Mr. Muranga wanted to know, "who might the kidnapped woman be?"

"I have an idea, but I suspect that Dr. Peel probably knows. Why not visit her?"

"Thank you, professor."

4

Four days later, Prof G received a call from Gillian herself. She began tentatively: they had not formally been introduced, but she had heard about him. He responded that he too had heard about her. Relieved, she came to her point: she would like to talk with him. Fine, he answered—did he assume correctly that it was urgent? Well, not *urgent*, but she knew it was the holidays, and she sort of wanted to actually see him before the university reopened. Yes, well, why didn't she drop by his house? Brilliant. Was he free this afternoon? Yes, this afternoon would be OK, and he gave her directions.

Promptly at three p.m., she was knocking at his gate. Prof G escorted her to the living room, where less than a week earlier he had discussed the kidnapping with Mr. Muranga. She chose one of the straight-backed wooden chairs, and Prof G sat in one of the stuffed chairs. Prof G's wife again brought in a thermos of tea and a plate of biscuits.

Gillian occupied herself with preparing her tea and choosing a biscuit. But she only took one sip. "A Mr. Muranga visited me while I was in the hospital," she began. "I understand you suggested he visit me."

"That's right." Prof G said. "I hope that was OK so soon after surgery. In fact, how did the surgery go?"

"No problem. My surgery was laparoscopic, so it didn't feel like a big deal." She paused. "He said you thought I might know who had been kidnapped with Lenny Mlongo."

Prof G nodded.

"You are exactly right. I came to explain to you, and see what I could do to sort of help. It should have been me, you know—" Her voice cracked, so she stopped and took another sip of tea. Then another biscuit.

Prof G waited.

"OK." She drew a breath and started again. "I don't know Dr. Linda Jankowski well, but I've recently been working with her now that MSF is in the District Hospital, and I've seen what an excellent doctor she is. So, when I found out about my bad Pap smears—did you know this part?" Prof G shook his head. "OK, I've had some abnormal Paps, I had a conization, then I was retested. Len says he's never seen the retests come back positive. Well, mine did. I had some biopsies, and this was real cervical cancer—very early stage, hadn't spread anywhere. But I still needed a hysterectomy.

"Anyway, when I talked with Linda a couple weeks ago, I hadn't had the biopsies yet. I talked to Len and he thought the retests were false positives. So I was telling Linda all this, and I invited her to come to Dadaab with us. She said, with the District so busy, she really couldn't get away. I could tell it wasn't something she sort of really wanted to do."

She took another sip of tea. "So, OK, the biopsies came back real cancer. And then I called Linda because…well, I don't know why. I guess I just wanted to talk to someone. I didn't ask her to go to Dadaab, but she told me she would go for me. Of course I told her I wasn't asking, she didn't need to, all that. But she didn't listen. She said she knew it was an important trip—she was right on that, actually—and that someone needed to go. She told me to just take care of what I needed to, and she'd check with Len. So I told her again that she didn't need to go, and then I thought she *did* listen. Maybe I'm fooling myself, but when I went to the hospital I wasn't worried about the trip—though I had also convinced myself that Linda hadn't gone."

Another pause. "So, when Mr. Muranga came and told me that Len had been kidnapped—that was the first I'd heard about the kidnapping—and did I know who might have been with him, well, of course I knew." Her voice was steady now, but a tear trickled down her left cheek. "So I came to tell you what I know, but I also want to tell you what I told Mr. Muranga: that I'll do whatever I can." She sniffed. "Whatever I can to get Len and Linda back." She set down her teacup and wiped her eyes roughly with her hands.

Now Prof G's dancing eyes glistened, and he reached out and gently touched her upper arm. "Thank you, Gillian," he said. "Thank you for that kind offer. I'm sure Mr. Muranga is in a far much better position to use that offer than I am, so I'm glad you told him." Then he sat back and said, "Let me tell you something different…" and with that he began a long story.

He told her that he was one of many children, and not the smartest one. But he had been named after an uncle, and so he in some way was supposed to *be* that uncle. That uncle had been a traditional healer and it had been determined that he too was to be a healer. By the time he was going to primary school, independence had come and East Africans were now going to medical school at Makerere University in Uganda. By the time he was finishing secondary school, there was a medical school in Nairobi. But all of this schooling—the secondary schooling, the university, the travel—all this took money and there was not enough for all of his brothers and sisters. However, he needed to follow his name, and his family knew they could not pay for all of his brothers and sisters to get that level of education. So he had been chosen; it was the family's plan. His older brothers had even paid his secondary school fees.

Today one of his sisters was a retired nurse; three of his brothers were farmers. One brother and another sister had been teachers. All were proud of him, but none wished that they walked in his shoes. He wasn't the smartest, he said again, but he was the one chosen to get a university education and all the responsibilities that followed—both to his family and his country. But all this, he said, was only because his family had used their meager resources on him.

At first, as Gillian listened to his tale, she was frustrated: why this tangent? Why weren't they talking about Len and Linda? But as Prof G finished, she realized what he was telling her. He was giving her the gift of shared experience: he too had had the awful experience of being the recipient of grace.

## 5

Just over two weeks after Leonard Mlongo had been kidnapped, Dr. Alan Hodges was still in Kenya. There were, of course, the ongoing negotiations for Mlongo's release, and, yes, the need for a temporary replacement. It was a big decision: the AIDS Institute's usual budget of twenty million dollars had quadrupled with the NMPSP activities and the new emphasis on all chronic diseases, and Dr. Hodges, as a board member, felt responsible. He also felt responsible because the AIDS Institute was his idea, he had been the first director, and it was through his influence and effort that the first funding had been found. He liked to think of it as a truly Kenyan organization, proven by Mlongo being the director. The absence of this decisive leader precipitated the need for decisive leadership, and Dr. Hodges provided it.

His first decision was easy: to suspend the NMPSP activities in the Dadaab area. Suspend, not cancel. He consulted with Dr. Peel who, to his surprise, readily agreed. His second decision was equally easy: to ensure that all AIDS treatment activities proceeded normally. He knew that disruption of ARV treatment would lead to drug resistance. It had already happened during the post-election violence, and he was determined it wouldn't happen again.

The harder decision was the NMPSP activities themselves in the rest of the country, and the chronic disease clinics the AIDS Institute had begun setting up. The Institute had been funded to coordinate NGO participation countrywide, yet the NMPSP had, in a sense, been targeted. If they suspended all screening activities, would that send the wrong message to Al Shabaab? If they continued, would that be insensitive to the families of those kidnapped, and put the other workers at risk? He decided to call a meeting of some key players who could help him decide: Dr. Peel, Dr. Kasamani from the St. Anthony's–District partnership, Dr. Hellen from the evaluation team, and Dr. Walt, who just happened to be back in Kenya, and had appointed himself point man for NMPSP kidnapping information for US partners.

Dr. Hodges convened the meeting in Mlongo's office. There were the two upholstered wooden armchairs in front of the desk, and two straight-backed wooden chairs, which he moved forward. While he was arranging the chairs, Gillian Peel walked in, followed shortly by Hellen. A few minutes later Kasamani came in, and the four settled themselves in the chairs in front of the desk. Then Walt burst in, filling the room with his apologies for being late. Seeing no open chair, he slid behind the desk and sat in Mlongo's wheeled desk chair.

Hodges briefly welcomed the group, and wasted no time on preliminaries: how did the group feel about continuing with NMPSP activities?

Walt spoke first. "Well, folks, it's really good to

be back with you all, though I know we all wish it was under different circumstances. I know you folks have been on the front lines here, and I want you to know that there are an awful lot of people back in the States praying, not just for Linda and Mlongo, but for wisdom for all of you as you face each decision. In my tradition we would begin a meeting like this with prayer; I wonder if any of you mind if I go ahead and do that?" No one voiced an objection, so Walt stood and unburdened himself of a heartfelt invocation, not only for the meeting ahead of them, but more especially for the safety and swift release of Doctors Linda Jankowski and Leonard Mlongo, as well as for wisdom for all those present as they had important decisions confronting them. And for the negotiators too, as they blah blah blah. The prayer lasted more than five minutes: Dr. Hodges was surreptitiously timing it, and was starting to wonder about the etiquette of interrupting a man's conversation with his God when Walt finally interrupted it himself. He sat down, took out a handkerchief, and dabbed at his brow.

"Thank you, Doctor…um…Jorgensen?" Dr. Hodges began.

"Oh yes," Walt said, "I guess we haven't actually met. I'm Walt Jorgensen from Evangel Hospital. I think I know everyone else here, except…" And he looked over at Kasamani, to whom he was duly introduced.

"Fine. Now to the main question again," Dr. Hodges continued. "Perhaps I could introduce a little context. Dr. Peel here and I have already discussed the Dadaab screening, and we both agree that it should be suspended for now. The question facing us is about all the other screening. Should we continue with business as usual? Yes, Kasamani?"

"You are quite right that this is a sensitive matter, and I suppose one way to think about it is to consider what Linda herself might recommend. Now it's true, she was not heavily involved in the St Anthony's–District partnership—at least as regards screening. But there was a very clear reason: she was busy at the District Hospital taking care of sick people, including people who had been referred in by the screening. It's also true that she was actually on a supervision trip when she was taken hostage. I think she would like to see the screening continue."

"That is a very reasonable approach, Kasamani, and I have to admit I'm leaning that way myself. Dr. Jorgensen, do you agree that we should continue with the screening?"

Walt agreed that, knowing Linda the way he did, and actually having known her for several years now, her self-effacement and humility were key personal characteristics—to say nothing of her amazing competence as a doctor. He opined that she would be quite embarrassed if some major change in policy was undertaken on her account, and quite agreed with Dr. Kasamani.

"Thank you, Dr. Jorgensen. Now if—"

"But I can't really say that I know Dr. Mlongo as well as I know Linda." Walt plowed on. "Of course I've been in meetings with him, as I guess all of us here have, but I don't really have enough experience with his program to even offer an educated opinion, so I'm going to have to leave that decision with people who knew him—or I guess I should say *know* him, shouldn't I?—better than I did."

"We'll do it," said Gillian.

"Yes," Dr. Hodges agreed. "We at the Institute have discussed this, and are already leaning in the direction of continuing with all screening activities. It sounds like this group, at least, is supportive. Hellen, is there anything in your evaluation so far that bears on this?"

"Only this, Alan," Hellen answered. "Of the now one million households screened so far, fully one third have been under programs coordinated by the AIDS Institute."

"Wow!" Walt said.

"And the only really successful public–private effort so far has been the St. Anthony's–District partnership, coordinated by Kasamani here. So if we just go by statistics, our colleagues who were kidnapped are connected with some of the pivotal efforts of the whole NMPSP."

Walt was nodding vigorously as Dr. Hodges granted that those statistics reinforced the consensus. "But there is one more thing I wanted to mention."

Hodges cleared his throat. "When we first met with the negotiator, Mr. Muranga, he asked those of us present to not discuss anything with the media—"

Walt started to answer the question that had not been asked of him, but this time Dr. Hodges went straight ahead through the intersection at the same speed, even though the light had turned yellow: "—for the safety of the hostages and their early release. His concern was that media attention would encourage the kidnappers to hold out for a higher ransom." He glanced at Walt to see if he was trying to nose into the traffic, and decided to let him in—after one more sentence: "The initial ransom demanded, I assume you all know, was one million dollars."

Walt had forgotten to downshift, so he lurched and bucked in third gear: "I'd just like to…uh, one *million* dollars? Well, I wasn't at that meeting with Mr. Mur—what is it?… The thing is…"

"The thing is simple, Walt," Gillian announced. "The ransom *was* one million dollars, but after your interview, broadcast nationally in the US and readily available here, the ransom was jacked up to two million. Thanks a lot."

The red patches spread from Walt's neck to his face.

Dr. Hodges wanted to make sure that everyone was on the same page, so to finish what he started he reiterated that there should be no further contacts with the media. Full stop. But Walt had not had *his* full stop, so he collected himself for *his* concluding statement. "It *is* all very tragic, and I would like to simply explain—"

"You blew it, Walt," Gillian said.

Hodges ignored Gillian, and addressed Walt. "Please go ahead, Dr. Jorgenson."

"OK, I'm sorry," Walt began. "The interview *segment* that appeared on TV was a fraction of what I said. That reporter asked me some good questions, but the most important parts of my answers didn't get broadcast. The thing was so heavily edited that they made it sound like it was about Somali Muslims kidnapping American Christians, and right at Christmastime too. But they took my words out of context! I had hoped that an international outpouring of sympathy would comfort them and maybe even lead to their release—"

"But you were wrong, Walt," Gillian said.

It was Kasamani who surgically staunched the flow of words. "We have come to an agreement about the NMPSP activities. We will work while we wait for the negotiations." He noticed the red return to Walt's neck. "Work while we wait. There is nothing else we can do."

**Somalia**

Gradually, Linda became aware of the sound of an engine—the low, rough rumbling of a diesel engine, coming closer. Her guards moved out of her doorway toward the front of the house, talking in low voices. Then she heard the sound of someone outside, or perhaps several people, creeping toward the front of the house. She heard the guards talking urgently with these others, and then they fell silent. The engine grew louder, and headlight beams flashed in the front room as the lorry turned and lurched toward the house.

A shout came from direction of the lorry. After that, she was sure of nothing, except that the first automatic weapon gunfire was very close, coming from the front of their house. It was answered by gunfire from the lorry. As bullets ripped whining and clawing through the house, she slid down flat on the floor and pushed herself toward the curtain. Mlongo was doing the same, so they both lay face down with the curtain between them. Mlongo reached his arm under the curtain and stretched it over her shoulders. They were both trembling.

The gunfire continued erratically, interspersed with cries and shouts and pounding footsteps. And then Linda gradually became aware that the gunfire was only coming from *there*, not *here*. And when the gunfire from *there* stopped, it was not answered by anything from *here*. Linda heard shouts coming from the direction of the lorry, getting closer, now accompanied by heavy footsteps. She tried to push herself deeper into the dirt floor, and felt Mlongo's arm tighten.

Suddenly, a new barrage of automatic gunfire

erupted, aimed at the shouts, and answered by more gunfire from the direction of the shouts. Now there was running—running away from the house, not toward it, and the sound of the lorry revving and speeding away, and another vehicle—or two or three—in pursuit. The gunfire continued, getting farther away. More lorries arrived, accompanied by more shouts, but no new gunfire. And then the shouts were gone, and the sounds of the lorries faded, and gunshots echoed far away until they sounded like toy guns. And after—was it thirty minutes, or three hours?—everything was quiet. Linda and Mlongo lay shivering on the dirt floor. As the quiet deepened, they stopped shivering, but didn't move apart.

Sometime later a rooster announced that they had come to the back side of night, but he got no response. A few minutes later he tried again, and another rooster staked his claim to the impending dawn. And then, very far away, the muezzin called the faithful to pray—and Linda and Mlongo stirred. Linda was stiff, and every movement made her muscles ache. But now, wide awake in the quiet, it hurt just as much not to move. So she slowly turned over and sat up, and Mlongo did the same. Cautiously, he lifted the curtain.

They were too afraid to talk. They sat, listening for any sound from the front room. There was none.

They waited as birds chirped outside and the pink glow of dawn seeped into the room. In the glow they saw something in the doorway at the other end of their chains—a motionless lump. Linda flexed her legs and the chain moved toward her, but still the lump did not move. Mlongo did the same, and his chain also moved freely. He slowly slid himself toward the front room. Arriving at the doorway, he peered cautiously through it, and then quietly said, "Linda." It sounded like a shout. "They're all dead. Come."

Linda scooted forward as well, and saw what Mlongo had seen: one of their guards lay face up in the doorway, dried blood on his chest and on the floor, his shirt and chest torn by bullets. The other guard lay face down in a pool of blood. Their AK-47s had fallen next to them on the floor. As the light increased, they saw more bullet holes in the house, both the outside wall and the one that separated them from the front room. Mlongo stood and hopped to the window. "There's more," he said. Linda joined him and looked out. Three bloody corpses lay scattered among the acacia trees.

For nearly a month Mlongo and Linda had not been asked, were not allowed, to make any choices, any decisions. It took them a few moments to realize that no one was going to tell them what to do; that they had to decide, to act. They had momentarily forgotten, too, that there was no longer a need to keep silent.

"How can we can get these cuffs off?" Mlongo began.

"Handcuffs must have a key," she said, and Mlongo knelt down next to the guard lying on his back—but did not immediately start feeling for the keys. He was looking for something else. "What is it?" she asked.

"Oh, just a habit, I guess. It's been drilled in to me not to touch blood without gloves on. But I suppose…"

Linda squatted on the other side of the body and started patting the pockets. "One effect of being trained before AIDS," she said, "is that I don't have that innate reaction. And I've got no cuts on my hands. And I sure want to get these cuffs off." She found a pocket with two small keys, and a minute later, for the first time in days, they could spread their chafed ankles.

Being able to separate their feet, to walk, suddenly seemed the most important skill a human could have. The moved through the whole house—there was nothing except their chains and the two dead teenagers with their guns. They had both seen many dead people; but those dead people had been on hospital beds, on trolleys in casualty, or in the morgue. Dead bodies did not belong on the floor of a mud-and-wattle house, or under the acacias in front. They knew they should leave, but they hesitated. They were programmed to act when people were horizontal and bloody: expose the wounds, check the vital signs, start the IVs…or call the morgue attendant. And, woven through all this, was the morbid fascination so many feel when passing a horrendous motor vehicle accident.

But these thoughts and feelings were brief, and remained unspoken. Mlongo was rapidly becoming again the decisive director he always tried to portray to the NGOs he'd worked for. "Well, we have no idea what just happened here—except that there's no one guarding us. So we either stay here and wait for somcone to find us, or we walk west toward Kenya. I don't know which is more dangerous: for someone to come back here and recapture us, or for us to start moving and be captured by someone else."

"But we're lost!" Linda said. A deep breath, and then: "We're dead no matter what we do, but I'm so tired of sitting, I'd be grateful for chance to walk—especially if we don't think that's any worse than just waiting."

"OK, sure. By the way, do you remember which direction that lorry drove off last night, when the other lorries came? I think—" but Linda was already turning toward the southeast "—yes, I think they went that way too. Another reason for us to go the opposite way, back to Kenya."

They had nothing to bring with them, so they walked out, past the three corpses in front of the house. The third one was face up: the tall guard from their previous place who'd had diarrhea. "Oh!" Linda started. They both stood for a moment, bowed their heads briefly, and continued onto a dirt track where, after a short distance, they saw where the lorry had been last night—and there was another dead body. And another. With that many dead from both sides, whatever the "sides" were, surely someone would be coming back, and they felt even more strongly that they did not want to be there. So they walked.

As they walked, they kept the sun toward their right or behind them. The dirt track wandered between bushes for perhaps half a kilometer, passing a few other mud-and-wattle buildings that seemed abandoned. Then they came to a larger dirt road, and without discussing it they turned left. The sun directly behind them cast long shadows on the road: two tall, skinny people out for an early-morning walk.

After they had walked for about an hour, and were starting to feel hot and thirsty, a pickup drove up from behind and stopped suddenly just in front of them, raising a huge cloud of dust. The driver was a middle-aged man with a red beard, and there were several cardboard boxes in the back. His passenger was a young man carrying an AK-47. Linda cringed, expecting to be shot, but nothing happened. There was no possibility of outrunning the pickup, so they walked up to the driver, who said only, "Get in." Mlongo asked in both English and Swahili where they were and where he was going, but the driver hit the wheel with his fist. "Get in!" he shouted, and the young man with the gun began waving it. They quickly climbed into the bed of the pickup, expecting to be driven back to the buildings they had just left.

But the sun stayed securely behind them. After several minutes the young man tapped on the back window, and started motioning vigorously with an outstretched palm. Linda caught it first: "He wants us to lie down." They flattened themselves on the corrugated bed of the pickup, and a minute later a lorry whizzed by in the other direction.

After about half an hour the pickup slowed, then stopped. The young man with the gun came back and motioned them to get out. For a moment they were hostages again, and acted like hostages: obedient. Then the young man pointed down the road and said, "Liboi." Linda stood motionless, but Mlongo grinned. "Liboi. We're in Kenya!" he told her. The young man dashed back into the pickup, which promptly sped off north.

# 6

Mr. Muranga was sitting that same morning in the otherwise empty Pumzika Club in the UN compound at Dadaab, talking—or rather bargaining—with a Somali man. Muranga was being polite, but firm. Two million, he was saying, was unreasonable, and he carefully spelled out the reasons why. First, the promised video had never appeared on Al Jazeera. Oh yes, yes, the Somali man had responded, dismissive of such a quibble. Meaning, Mr. Muranga pressed on, that proof that the hostages were alive must precede *any* further negotiating. As he said this he looked up—he was facing the door—and saw a large GSU officer in combat fatigues motioning to him. He excused himself momentarily and walked to the door to see what the GSU officer wanted. Standing next to him were an ungroomed Kenyan man and an equally ungroomed grey-haired white woman. The GSU officer identified the pair to Mr. Muranga as doctors Leonard Mlongo and Linda Jankowski.

Mr. Muranga was unable to say a word for a full ten seconds. Then he gave an abrupt laugh, greeted them, and said he thought it would be important for them, and the GSU officer, to meet a certain Al Shabaab representative he had just been conversing with. He led them all back into a now very empty Pumzika Club, with only a half cup of tea where the Al Shabaab representative had been sitting. They went to the bar and called for the waiter, who had not seen anyone leave. The GSU officer called in two colleagues who, being given a description of the Al Shabaab man by Mr. Muranga, went looking. Meanwhile Mr. Muranga ordered four more cups of tea, and he and the GSU officer listened to the whole story from Linda and Mlongo. Mr. Muranga took copious notes.

"And you were not beaten, tortured, or otherwise harmed at any point?" Mr. Muranga wanted to confirm.

No, they assured him, there was no physical harm. "But," Linda offered, "I wouldn't mind a shower, some food, and maybe a change of clothes."

"Of course," Mr. Muranga assured them. "All of the things you both left in your rooms here at the UN compound have been kept securely under lock and key, and you will be promptly issued them."

"And maybe a telephone?" Mlongo suggested.

"But of course." Just as they were finishing, the two GSU colleagues came in with a Somali man in handcuffs.

"We found your man," they announced to Mr. Muranga. The handcuffed man looked annoyed; Mr. Muranga looked puzzled.

"This gentleman," he said, "is not the man I was just bargaining with."

"Noted," one of them said. "We will detain him for further questioning."

The four then stood to leave, and the GSU officer

requested that they submit a formal police report. Linda and Mlongo agreed, and Mr. Muranga promised to get them on the flight to Nairobi that evening.

# 7

Gillian and Hodges were there to meet the plane. Gillian said nothing; she simply swallowed Linda in a long, tight hug. Hodges pumped Mlongo's hand, and he too had trouble knowing what to say. Words flowed a little easier when Gillian hugged Mlongo and Hodges shook Linda's hand. Mlongo's wife, Monica, had stayed with the children, and decided to wait the extra day back at the Institute. The next morning they all flew back to the School of Medicine together. Linda wanted to go right to the District, but agreed to stop in with Mlongo at the AIDS Institute.

The Institute driver had picked them up at the airport, and as they drove up to the Institute they saw a large crowd on the sidewalk. When they stopped, two security guards snapped to attention and saluted, stamping once with their right foot. As Linda and Mlongo came out of the vehicle, another guard stopped them from moving until a fourth guard had finished rolling a red carpet across the sidewalk from the lobby of the Institute, stopping just short of their vehicle. They were then allowed to proceed, accompanied by applause and cheering and ululation. Mlongo nodded graciously; Linda turned red. She felt like she was getting married all over again—an arranged marriage this time.

They were ushered upstairs to the large boardroom. The conference tables had been removed and replaced with chairs; there were fifty people in the room, TV cameras, photographers, and a church choir. This isn't necessary, Linda thought, doing her best to look gratified. They were escorted to a small platform at the front, and Linda looked over the sea of faces. Kasamani was there, and behind him old van der Stoeckle sat grinning. Over to the left she saw Walt, who stood up as soon as they made eye contact, then sat down again. She recognized several more faces from St. Anthony's, and Prof G sat over on the right.

When Dr. Hodges called the gathering to order, the choir stopped as two dozen raised cellphones were snapping pictures. A TV cameraman moved forward and thrust a huge microphone in his face. Hodges said they had come together for one simple reason: to pay tribute to their colleagues, Doctors Mlongo and Jankowski, who were now free people. The crowd erupted. This was a day of celebration, he said (inducing piercing ululation), and he wondered if perhaps one or both of the doctors had something to say. Linda was relieved when Mlongo stood.

"Good morning," he began, and the crowd bellowed back, "GOOD MORNING!"

"We are *so* glad to be here." Again the crowd

erupted. "To be here, and not in Somalia. We are so grateful for your welcome."

"What was it like there?" the television reporter interrupted. "Were you tortured?"

"No," Mlongo answered, "we were treated all right."

"In what kind of place were you held?" another reporter asked.

Hodges rescued him then, and said there would be time later to review all that. This was simply a welcome back.

"Yes," Mlongo said, "I'm sure you can appreciate that now I just wanted to spend time with my family, and then get back to work." The crowd applauded as he moved to the front row, hugged his wife and children, and joined them there.

Hodges then turned toward Linda. Did she have anything to say? Not really, she admitted. Well, would she at least come and greet the crowd? She reluctantly stood, and as she did so, she saw Dr. Ng'etich in the back of the room, looking earnest and relieved, and beside him Salome. She waited until the room was quiet, and until she knew she could speak without her voice cracking. "We…well, I…I have never been welcomed home like this before. I don't really know what to say." She paused, and there was scattered applause. "I just wish there was some way to channel all this energy for…for the work that all of us have ahead of us, here in Kenya." Awkward silence. "We weren't killed, we weren't hurt…there wasn't even any ransom paid. So…" She looked across the upturned faces, all waiting to see where she was going, but even she didn't know. "So, anyway," she concluded awkwardly, "thank you for welcoming us home. Thank you so much."

When she sat down, the choir started singing, and once again the crowd was comfortable.

<br>

## 8

Later that day, Linda was driven to St. Anthony's Hospital. It was, she hoped, her last welcome home. She had wanted to go directly to the District, but St. Anthony's, it seemed, did not want to accept that she no longer worked there. There were fortunately no banners on the hospital gate—though it was repainted, as was the administration wing, and there were freshly cultivated flowers blooming along the entrance drive. Kasamani and van der Stoeckle escorted her directly to the male ward, where new copper tubing had been installed along the inner walls, bringing oxygen to each bed. There were also now curtains between the beds, new mosquito nets, and IV poles on the floor instead of bent wires dangling from the rafters for hanging IV bottles.

"St. Anthony's is welcoming you home," van der Stoeckle announced, and grinned.

"Well, thank you. It's really good to be back."

The grin on van der Stoeckle's face remained. "You

are aware, I'm sure, of the history of St. Anthony himself?"

Linda admitted that she hadn't recently reviewed the history of the saints, but seemed to remember that there was more than one St. Anthony.

"Quite right!" And the grin got bigger. "But now we are thinking of St. Anthony of Padua, who is the patron saint of lost items. You were a lost item, and now you are found. Ha ha!"

"Well, um, thank you, I guess." She looked around. "I see that you've made some changes here."

"This is what I am telling you from the beginning. We have a *new* St. Anthony's, but we are only starting. You will be seeing so much more. Now the doctors are going to be very comfortable when they make rounds."

"The *doctors* are going to be comfortable?" Linda laughed. "I thought the idea was to make the *patients* comfortable."

"But doctors are comfortable when the patients are comfortable, isn't it?"

"Yes, I suppose. How about if I walk around a bit here and see your changes. Then I do need to get on to the District." She walked through the male ward and flipped through several charts. After glancing at the first half dozen, she realized that this *was* a new St. Anthony's. The second patient she saw was a middle-aged man with lower-back pain from sciatica, uncommon in her experience for hospitalized patients. Then there was an elderly man with a heart attack, proven by ECG—again, unusual for this part of Kenya.

But when she walked to the end of the ward, she wasn't sure if things really were different. The last cubicle, the one with AIDS patients, seemed depressingly familiar—although now there was a true isolation area created on what had been the back porch of the ward.

Her biggest surprise was on the pediatric ward: there were only five patients, and two were in traction for femur fractures. She commented on this to the nurse. Was it always this empty? Oh no, the nurse assured her. It was simply the dry season with not much malaria. But we used to get twenty patients during this season, and fifty during malaria peaks, Linda remembered. What happened? The nurse wasn't sure. What about the District Hospital? Well, yes, the nurse admitted that she had heard the District pediatric ward remained crowded.

She spotted Kasamani in the hallway and went over to him.

"What do you think of the changes?" he asked.

"Interesting, the patients that are here," she said. "I noticed more diabetics just now on the ward than I remember from before. And one with gall bladder disease, and a guy with a heart attack—it's beginning to look like the sort of patients I saw in medical school in the US."

"Yes, that is interesting—and supports what the

epidemiologists have been telling us, that Kenya is in the epidemiological transition, moving from the so-called third world diseases to the Western diseases."

"But within the two-month time span since I've been gone?"

Kasamani laughed. "Well, not within two months! But if you've actually noticed a difference, I wonder how much that has to do with the screening? The St Anthony's–District partnership has been very successful, and maybe it's been uncovering all these folks who up until now haven't been getting treatment. I guess that's the whole reason it was started, to highlight and then fill in a major gap in Kenyan health care."

That afternoon Linda really returned home to the District Hospital. She wanted first to thank Ng'etich for coming to her welcoming at the AIDS Institute. She found him at the nurses' station of the delivery room, writing a note in the file of a patient on whom he had just performed a vacuum delivery. "Linda! Welcome home!"

"Thanks Ng'etich—and thank you for coming to the Institute to welcome me."

"Sure. By the way, did you know that we can now do vacuum deliveries here? An MSF midwife likes using the machine, and I've done two already this week."

"Excellent. I hope the apparatus won't disappear when MSF goes." Ng'etich looked up and cocked his head at Linda. "Oh yes," she continued, "when I first came, we had the vacuum extractors here, and I used them a lot. I never found out what happened to them. So, how is the rest of the hospital?"

"Oh, about the same, I guess," he said.

"Busy?"

"Very."

"Well then," Linda continued, "do you see many patients coming in from the NMPSP program?"

"There might be in outpatient, but I don't get there very much because I'm mostly on the wards."

"So the sorts of patients on the wards haven't changed?"

"Not that I can tell."

"And pediatrics…? I just came from St. Anthony's, where they have five patients on the ward, and two of them are in traction. How's the ward here?"

"I hardly get to pediatrics anymore. MSF usually puts a doctor there, but their last one left last week and the new one hasn't come yet. I think the clinical officer has been seeing those patients, though. I've got a minute now. Let's go look."

When they arrived at the ward, they found the chaos Linda remembered: children squalling, a crowd of mothers around the nurses' station, and the blaring television. Linda's question might have been answered, but she could not get away. "Daktari!" A nurse rushed up to them. "Oh, both of you are here. It's good you have come. There is a child collapsing just here." And indeed, a six-month-old was gasping when they arrived at the bedside. Someone produced a pediatric-sized Ambu bag that fit perfectly, but it was too late. "And while you are here, Daktaris," the nurse murmured, touching Linda's shoulder. And Linda and Ng'etich spent the next hour and a half reviewing patients, making suggestions, changing some orders… Documenting the chaos.

*

Finally, Linda walked home, past the still-empty gigantic billboard frame, mulling on the day's events while dancing out of the way of a swerving *matatu*. She passed the motorcycle taxis still waiting for passengers, and turned off the main road. She was suddenly back to work, wondering why that last kid had such a swollen belly, wondering if she and Ng'etich had worked long enough trying to resuscitate that six-month-old.

She wondered all the way until she arrived at the place where they made bricks. Another huge pile of stacked bricks had dried in the sun, and was now awaiting burning. Yes, things were a bit better at the District, but how long would MSF be propping up the place? A small boy scampered up to her, grinning proudly. "I'm fine," he said.

"Well, so am I," she said. "I think." She continued her walk, and the small boy grabbed her hand to accompany her. His hand was sticky, but this was his welcome to her, so she stuck to him. And continued mulling. She had been kidnapped working for a screening program she didn't believe in, kidnapped for no reason, and had eventually just walked away: no rescue, no ransom. What was the point? What good did all that do? The small boy unstuck himself and scurried back to his play.

How does any of this help anyone? she wondered. Am I supposed to be different because of all of this? What do I have to offer? She stopped and turned. The small boy was sauntering along behind her, dragging a stick and studying the trail it left in the path. Yes, what do I have to offer? And she was immediately back at the mass she had been to shortly after Mercy died. It had been so unsatisfying. She went to mass to get outside of herself, but that day it seemed she only sank in deeper. The homily was boring, the offertory song proclaimed her own horrible mistake, and that little boy with the egg, the broken egg... She wiped her sticky hand on her slacks.

But there was something else about that mass. What was it? She started humming the tune of the offertory song, then singing:

*Nikupe nini ee Bwana, sina cha kukupa wewe,*
*Sadaka niliyo nayo sio ya kupendeza.*
What can I give you, O Lord? I haven't anything to give you.
The offering I have is not pleasing.

It was such a bouncy, driving tune that she kept singing:

*Ni wakati wa sadaka moyo unahofu*
*Maana sina cha kukupa ewe Mungu wangu*
*Na tazame wenzangu wote kutolea zawadi kubwa*
*Kasoro mimi tu sina cha kutoa.*
It is the time of offering, but my heart fears
Because I haven't anything to give you, O my God.
I see all these people offering large gifts;
My lack is that I alone have nothing to offer.

But my goodness, the lyrics! How can I sing about my offering not being pleasing, about having nothing to offer, and feel so comforted by the tune? There was something else in that mass. Maybe it's in every mass… She stopped. Ng'etich was at that mass—I remember, it was the first time I'd seen him at mass. But was it the mass itself, or was it what I did with it? She continued walking, then stopped again. OK, it sounds foolish, but I need to see if Ng'etich remembers that mass.

She turned and walked back to the hospital. As she entered the compound, Ng'etich was just coming out the front door. She grabbed his hand and pulled him toward the tree with the bench under it; the bench where he had set up his outdoor clinic during the protests.

"Ng'etich, you remember that mass we went to just after Mercy died? The one where that little boy broke the egg? You were there, right?"

He looked puzzled.

"OK, I know you were there, because just before I came in, I saw you walk up toward the front. It was a mass led by children, and they were the ones who offered the prayers after we sang the creed. Some of them were so small you couldn't even see them behind the podium. You remember?"

"The one where all those little kids brought their small-small offerings up to the altar?"

"Yes, exactly. And we sang '*Ni wakati wa sadaka moyo unahofu / Maana sina cha kukupa ewe Mungu wangu.*' You remember?"

"Oh, yes. They came one by one with a bottle of Fanta and a mango and a bar of soap."

"Yes, yes. And the egg. Do you remember the one with the egg?"

"I think so."

"OK. This one little fellow had a big egg—a duck egg, I think—and the kids were all bunched together, you remember that? And this fellow with the egg carried it so seriously and so carefully, but just when he got to the altar, he fell and smashed his egg. You remember that, don't you? It was horrible, and he started crying and crying, and I went away feeling so terrible. But just now I remembered that mass, and even though I was so unsatisfied, something about it stays with me. And that song about having nothing to offer God… why does it have such a nice tune? Do you remember that mass?"

As Linda talked, Ng'etich's face betrayed little, except that he was following her story closely. When she stopped, he nodded. "But you didn't finish the story," he said.

"What do you mean?" she asked. "That's all I remember. Was there something else? What else?"

"You are right," he said. "I remember that small boy with the egg—the one who got knocked down and broke his egg and started wailing. And don't you remember? The priest picked up that little boy and then—while the choir kept singing and the small girls kept dancing—he held him to his chest, held him and rocked him while he cried, and all the rest of the kids had to wait to present their gifts. Maybe you couldn't see that in the back. And that boy cried and cried until he finally stopped. And the priest held him out straight in front of him and the small boy sniffed. I couldn't see the boy's face, but the priest smiled at him and then put him down. But that smile stayed on the priest's face, and the egg stain from the boy's shirt stayed on the front of his robes for the rest of the mass."

As Ng'etich recounted the incident, Linda heard a new story. She knew she had been there, knew he was retelling the same story she remembered, but now it was complete. When he finished, she was holding his hand with both of hers, and her face was, once again, washed with tears.

# Return to Laughter

**1**

It was a Saturday morning early in April, and the rains were just starting. The Friday afternoon downpour had caught Linda on her way back from the hospital, and then a steady rain had kept up half of the night. But the morning was bright and cool—too tempting, despite the sloppy roads, for Linda to forgo her weekly hourlong walk. She had returned home with brown stains on the cuffs of her jeans, and was sitting on her front steps digging the mud out of her soles with a stick. Halfway through the second shoe she heard honking outside her compound gate—unusual, as she lived near the end of her lane and none of her usual visitors had cars. Before she had both shoes back on the honking erupted again, and she shuffled to the gate with the laces untied. When she swung the gate open, an enormous Prado accelerated into her tiny compound. Walt opened the driver's door and shouted, "I'll bet you're wondering what I'm doing here! Well, I'll tell you in just a minute."

He turned off the engine, and as he got out, the other door opened and a tall young man in a safari suit with two cameras around his neck also got out. He had chaotic sandy hair and impossibly blue eyes. "Let me first introduce you to my friend Ian," Walt continued. "He's an Aussie photojournalist."

The young man came around the car and shook Linda's hand. "Noice to meet you," he said, and without waiting for a response went to the back seat and extracted two large leather shoulder bags.

"Ian's work is incredible," Walt said. "He's been covering the birth of the new South Sudan, and some of the images he's brought back…well, they cut right through you. Unforgettable. There's such poverty there, but the church growth continues to be absolutely phenomenal. Ian has an eye for that sort of thing. I call it 'Pictures of the Wind.' Why, you might ask. Remember how in John it says the Spirit moves like the wind and we can hear it but we don't know where it comes from and where it's going? But we sure can see what the wind does, can't we? So Ian here has been documenting what the Wind of the Spirit does. Pictures of the Wind."

"Well, I'm sure those pictures are very moving. Will you excuse me if I sit down here and tie my shoes?"

"No, no, go right ahead. So, about what I'm doing here. OK, so in all the many times I've come to Africa, I've spent most of my time in our 'Shangri La'"—with finger quotes—"at Evangel Hospital, or at other centers of power. Suddenly, it hit me like a ton of bricks how, you know, *insular* we can get, almost stuck in our own little worlds. How we stay in our, in our…" He held up his caved hands as if cradling a ball.

"Comfort zones?" Linda suggested as she stood up again.

"Exactly. So, I realized that traveling outside my comfort zone is actually to my advantage. It helps to, you know, broaden me. I decided to start getting outside Evangel Hospital. Getting out for my own good. And there's really no reason for this Catholic–Protestant split between church hospitals, don't you think? So I came to learn from you."

"OK." Linda was not at all sure what he wanted to learn, especially from the District Hospital. "So…"

"But you know," he plowed on, "I decided this back before the holidays, and before your, um…experience as a hostage."

Ian, his back toward the still-open gate, was snapping pictures of Linda and Walt talking, with her house in the background. He started moving closer to them. "So I guess that sort of trumps everything else, doesn't it?"

"Not really."

"Wow. Did you hear that, Ian? That's incredible, Linda. Here you were captured by Muslim fundamentalists while you were working to bring health care to those same Muslims—in the name of Christ, if I know you at all. You could have been tortured and killed, you escaped from a vicious gunfight—and you say that does *not* trump your ongoing work to bring quality health care to the Kenyans you've been committed to for over twenty years. Twenty years, Ian!" Ian moved in for some close-ups. "You know, most people would call what you did heroic."

"I can honestly say, Walt, that I have no idea what you're talking about."

"And with humility to boot! You're making my case stronger with everything you say."

"Now hold on, Walt. And Ian, I wonder if you could not stand right in front of me—in fact, could you just hold it with the pictures? Thanks. Let's back up a little, Walt, so at least we're talking about the same story. So, first, we weren't bringing health care to Muslims, we were visiting a Somali refugee camp on behalf of the screening program. And since I try to follow Jesus, I suppose everything I do is in the name of Christ—but I don't advertise that. In fact, I doubt I've ever put those words on it."

"No, no, of course not. Actions speak louder than words, don't they?"

"And we weren't captured by Muslim fundamentalists, we were captured by a couple of Somali teenage... well, pirates. They never talked to us about Islam."

"They didn't need to; they wanted the hostage money to further their brand of fundamentalism, don't you think?"

"I have no idea, because they never got the money. And of course we were *not* tortured or killed, and we did *not* escape from a vicious gunfight. We were lying on that dirt floor scared out of our wits. I don't think I could have moved even if you'd told me the house was on fire. I don't know how long we waited after the gunfire stopped, but it could have been hours. And when we finally got up and looked around, there was no one to escape from—except dead people. We just walked away."

"I'd call that heroic."

"I'd call it meaningless."

"Have you thought of writing up your story, and maybe submitting it to a magazine for publication?"

"No."

"Let me encourage you to do that, Linda." He leaned closer, and she could smell sour coffee on his breath. "This is an amazing opportunity to give our particular Christian spin on a very current global health issue. Two issues, really: the kidnapping by Muslim fundamentalists *and* the screening program itself. In fact, I can see a good book coming out of this, one that really would sell because the story is so gripping, but at the same time could educate people about global health—and, most important, spread the Gospel. And of course Ian here could do some incredible professional photos for the book."

Ian had been rummaging around in the back of the

Prado, and emerged with a large video camera on his shoulder. As he aimed it at them, Linda said, "Excuse me, Walt." She walked into her house and pulled the door closed behind her.

Ten minutes later she heard a knock at the door, and Walt's voice: "Linda, are you OK in there?" She had spent most of the time pacing, trying to erase both her anger toward Walt and her guilt for not inviting him in. She had just sat down to read when the knock came.

She went to the door. "Not exactly, Walt. I'm not sure what you've come here for, but I find it very distracting to try and have a conversation when someone is sticking a camera in my face. Now, if you'd both like to come in, I'd be glad to fix tea for all of us—but Ian has to leave his weapons at the door."

"Well, thank you, Linda—if it's not too much trouble." He turned around. "Ian?" Ian, whether feeling it was too much trouble, or unable to leave his weapons at the door, chose to sit in the Prado.

Walt leaned in the doorway to the kitchen. "I don't want to take a lot of your time because I know how busy you are, but if you could just—"

Linda turned from putting the kettle on the stove. "Walt," she interrupted, "it's Saturday and I am not overworked, as you can see. I don't know what stories you've heard about our time in Somalia—or who told them to you—but it seems to me you're talking nonsense. You said you came here to learn. I'm not a teacher, but at least I know what happened to me and what didn't. I don't know what it all means, what I'm supposed to learn from it, and all that. But there's no story to publish, no book to write, OK?"

"Well, it's certainly your story, Linda, but it just seems to me you don't want to hide your light under a bushel, you know." Linda retreated into preparing two cups of tea as Walt waited for her to take her light out from under the bushel. "Linda, I don't understand why you're so shy about this. You've got to believe in yourself. Don't keep putting yourself down; you're depriving the rest of us of what you have to offer."

Linda's hands were shaking as she put the mugs on the table, and some of the milky tea sloshed onto the scratched wood. She went into the kitchen to fetch a cloth. "So it's my fault that I don't understand what happened to me?" she said in a steely monotone as she mopped up the tea. She remained standing. "And somehow you find deep spiritual meaning in all of this—meaning that God forgot to tell me, is that it?"

"No, no, Linda, you don't get it. I'm just—" Walt's neck started turning red.

"No Walt!" Linda shouted. "*You* don't get it! You barge into my compound with that Ian fellow, who starts taking pictures of me without asking my permission—"

"Well, he—"

"And you tell me you want to learn from me—"

"I do—"

"—but spend all your time telling me what my story means, and then insult me by telling me *I'm* the one who's missing something because I don't see this deep spiritual meaning."

"No, it's only that—"

"Walt, shut *up*!" Linda stood with both hands on the table, glowering at Walt, whose face was now as red as his neck. He stared at the floor somewhere beyond Linda. The mugs of tea shivered. "Is somebody paying you to write this story? What's behind this?" Walt had been told to shut up, and he decided to stay that way. Linda felt her heart beating fast; she stopped, breathed deeply, and spoke more quietly.

"OK, Walt, I don't know why you think our kidnapping is so important, or why you think it's a story the world should know. But it's *not* a Christian–Muslim story, it's not a story of heroism—I was there; I know—and it really has nothing to do with health care. It's like if I was driving too fast, skidded, flipped my car over, and it rolled into a tree, and I walked out because I had been wearing my seatbelt. That sort of thing happens all the time. It's fortunate that in Somalia we didn't get hurt…but it has no more meaning than flipping my car over."

As the pause lengthened, Walt finally looked up.

"I actually wish it *did* have some meaning," she said finally, looking out the window. "I wish that this thing gave me some insight into how I can live in this…

this…what do you call it—'resource-constrained' situation. Not even fix it, just *live* with it." She came back to Walt. "But the one thing I *am* sure of is that I do not want you to publish any article or book about this. And Ian should delete all those pictures he took. I can see nothing beneficial coming out of some media-warped version of this story. Let Mlongo tell the story if anyone does—it's his screening program, his country."

Linda sat, and they both stared at their tea. "And there's another thing. I don't know if you heard about this, but a month or so before I went to Dadaab with Mlongo, I lost a patient. In fact, she was a woman who had worked for me in my house, cleaning and cooking and so on, for twenty years."

"I'm sorry, Linda. That's hard."

"Yes it is—but not only was she my patient, and someone I had known longer than anyone else here; she died because of a mistake I made." And she briefly told him the story. For just a moment, Linda saw another Walt. Some mask fell away, and Linda saw kicked-in-the-nuts pain, and then a fleeting look, not of blame, but of empathy. But she also saw that since Walt had no words for what was behind the mask, he felt exposed, naked. She looked away, embarrassed, and continued: "So Walt, there's this other story I'm living with, but the meaning is unfortunately much clearer. We try to help, all of us do, and sometimes we just plain make things worse."

The mask was back up, and she could see Walt working on a response, but she had no more energy to keep going. "Tell you what, Walt. Let's just stop here. I'm sure you'll be able to explain to me how we don't *have* to make things worse and all that—and I'll say, 'But we do make things worse,' and you'll say, 'But we don't have to.'" Linda forced a grin, and Walt's response was an authentic 'I get it' grin. She smiled. "I guess we're not in the mood for tea."

"No, I guess not," Walt said, unsure of what to do with his tea, his hands, himself.

"So let's at least go out to the Prado to show Ian we haven't torn each other to pieces."

**2**

That same Saturday evening, Mlongo was sitting with KK at a table at the Meating Place, a *hoteli* ten minutes' walk from the School of Medicine. Even though it was on the edge of downtown, the compound had several large trees, and each table was in its own grass-roofed gazebo. It was already dark, the *nyama choma* was on its way, and they were sipping their drinks—Mlongo a Tusker, KK a black-cherry Fanta. "Black-cherry Fanta?" Mlongo said. "What are black cherries, anyway?"

"*Prunus serotina*, a large North American cherry with an astringent fruit."

Mlongo had to swallow his sip quickly so he wouldn't lose it when he laughed. "How do you know this sort of thing, KK? Do you have an encyclopedia next to your bed?"

"No, just a dictionary. You can get a lot of what you need from a good dictionary, you know."

Mlongo had spent the afternoon with KK and Hellen, analyzing their statistics on screening, on changes in district and mission hospital clinic attendances and in-patient censuses, and on the focus groups to flesh out those statistics. They had gone far with no interruptions—it was, after all, Saturday—but Mlongo decided at six p.m. that he'd had enough. He dragged KK to the Meating Place, and Hellen said she might drop by later.

"A dictionary by your bed. That's remarkable, KK—and a little crazy, don't you think?"

"I actually do some of my best thinking at night. I even have these index cards…"

"Your index cards are famous, KK." As he reached for his Tusker, he saw Prof G coming up to the gazebo. "Hey, Prof, do you know when KK does his best thinking?"

"Yes," Prof G said, eyes twinkling. "At night. And he writes those thoughts on index cards he keeps next to his bed." He ducked into the gazebo and shook hands with Mlongo and KK. KK took the small pile of cards from his breast pocket and fanned them as proof.

"Now Prof, I'm surprised to see you here. It's well known that you are opposed to alcoholic beverages." Mlongo grinned.

"Now who told you that? I'm not *opposed* to alcoholic beverages, I just don't drink them. But didn't you look at the name of this *hoteli*? It's the Meating Place, not the Drinking Place. I'm a Kenyan, Mlongo. Of course I take *nyama choma*—and I take it with orange Fanta."

"Well then, Prof, sit down and join us."

"Fine. Now, I just saw Kasamani on the other side there…"

"Let him come too." Mlongo ordered a Fanta for Prof and a Tusker for Kasamani. More chairs came, more handshakes, more greetings.

The first order of *nyama choma* arrived on a ravaged wooden board, a hillock of salt on one corner. "Kasamani," Mlongo said, dipping a scrap of fatty goat into salt, "I haven't seen you in some time. You are still at the District?"

"Yes—'Under New Management,' as the petrol stations say," answered Kasamani around a mouthful of goat. "But in fact I haven't really spoken with you since your little episode up in Northeastern. If they starved you then, it seems you have very much recovered."

"Ah, you should have seen me up there. I was nothing more than a skeleton."

"*Ati* skeleton," said KK. "You surely must have put

back all your weight on the trip from Dadaab back to here. I don't remember any skeleton, and all I see now is a prominent Public Opinion."

"You see," Mlongo went on, "they have a great shortage of *nyama choma* and Tusker in Somalia. But yes, I am not suffering now," he said, and patted his Public Opinion.

Hellen joined the group. "You fellows just can't stay away from each other, can you? You work on Saturday afternoon, then you work on into the night over Tusker?"

"Let me assure you," Prof G said, "that this is not a working meeting. We are, on the contrary, celebrating Mlongo's growing waistline after he was starved in Somalia."

"Starved in Somalia? He did nothing but eat up there."

"Come sit, Hellen," said Mlongo. "Your Tusker and more *nyama choma* are on the way. And you are right—there was very little to do up there but eat and sleep."

"You're saying it was a vacation?" Kasamani asked.

"Sure," KK said. "He vacated his job here—I guess that's a vacation."

"We could set up a company," Hellen suggested, "and call it Desert Vacations. Provide your own transport to Dadaab, and we do the rest."

"All meals, lodging, and transport included," said Mlongo. "Armed security guards accompany you on every outing. Consistent daily schedules designed with your small party in mind."

"Enjoy cross-border excursions into Somalia—no need for a visa," Hellen continued.

"Sign me up," said Kasamani. "But what happened to you up there? I haven't heard—but maybe you've already told these guys."

"All we've done together since he got back is work," said KK. "We know as much as you do."

"Oh, there's not really much to tell," said Mlongo as more Tuskers, more Fantas, and more *nyama choma* came. "So we were two, you know. I was with Linda Jankowski—you work with her, don't you, Kasamani?"

"Oh yes, for years. She's still at the District. A very dedicated, very serious doctor. But she doesn't talk much about it. Seems it frightened her, maybe still worries her, I don't know."

"Yes, we had quite a bit of time together. But that last day." He laughed. "Oh dear, that *daktari*…" He laughed again, sat back, and took a sip of his Tusker. "So, you know these teenage boys captured us in Ifo, up there in Dadaab, and for nearly a month—it was over the holidays—we were together with Linda in a house somewhere in Somalia. Then on the very last day they loaded us into the back of a lorry and brought us somewhere else—we still have no idea why. Then they put us in the back of some dark hut, and since we were chained—"

"You were chained? What do you mean chained?" Kasamani asked.

"Well, OK—I had handcuffs around my ankles, and they were connected by a long chain to my guard who stayed in the front room. It was the same for Daktari—only she had her own guard. Oh yes, and there was some kind of curtain between Daktari and me, so we were separated. We got there maybe just before dark, and those guards were more nervous than the first guards we'd had. I tell you, I thought we were finished then. I thought we would never get out—you know, two teenage boys with AKs who are jumpy…"

"You thought it was over," Hellen said.

Mlongo laughed. "Finished! I knew it was over for us. I don't know about Daktari, but me, I figured this was the end. So, for a long time we were just there—it must have been hours. And then, I tell you…oh, it was terrible. Terrible!" He laughed. "There was loud gunfire, right next to us, and bullets everywhere, whizzing even through the hut we were in. So we lay down flat, but I knew one of those bullets would get us. I knew it."

"F in F," said KK.

"What? What's that, KK?"

"F in F. Feces in the fan."

"Oh, absolutely," laughed Mlongo. "Feces in the fan! That's what it was. It went on and on. I don't know how long it lasted, but there was nothing, *nothing* we could do. And then—now listen to this—the gunfire stopped, and though we weren't dead—"

"You were still very much alive," said Kasamani.

"Oh yes, very much alive, only that wasn't the end, because then we heard more lorries and more people, and they were coming toward us, and we knew we had survived only to be killed in the next round. So we just waited to be shot, or to be recaptured. But either way," he laughed, "we were finished."

Hellen smiled and shook her head. "Those guys were really playing with you."

"It was something, I tell you. So then there was more gunfire and more shouts and more lorries gunning their engines—more F in F—" He looked at KK, who nodded sagely as everyone else hooted. "And we knew again it was the end for us."

"That was it," laughed Kasamani. He wiped one palm across the other. "You were finished."

"This went on, oh, I don't know how long, hours anyway, most of the night, it seems, because after it stopped we were afraid to do anything, and we waited until…well, until the cocks started crowing."

"You were there all night."

"The whole night, lying on that dirt floor with Daktari, too afraid to move anywhere." And Mlongo laughed again. "But now listen. It was Daktari who moved first. She started pulling the chains, and when it seemed those guards didn't do anything, we slid ourselves into the front room—we couldn't walk, you know, because our ankles were handcuffed—so we slid in and found those fellows very much dead, AKs on the ground next to them. Then I stood up and hopped toward the front window—"

"Your feet were cuffed together." Hellen laughed as she imagined the scene. "And you stood up and jumped like a frog." She demonstrated by jumping with her feet together.

"Like a frog!" said Kasamani.

"Oh yes," said Mlongo. "So I jumped to the front window, and I saw more dead fellows out there—but there was no one to stop us from leaving."

"You were on your own," Prof G suggested.

"We were very much on our own then, Prof, but you see we had a problem. We couldn't walk. We had these handcuffs on our ankles, and all we could do is jump like frogs. So Daktari says, 'You know,' she says, 'handcuffs must have keys.' And we figured those dead guys on the ground must have the keys in their pockets. But there was blood all over the place, some of it still wet, and—well, you know it's automatic that you put on gloves before you touch anything with blood. Now of course we had no gloves, and before I could do anything, there is Daktari, kneeling down by one of those dead guys, feeling around in his pockets for the keys. And then she says, 'I was trained before there was AIDS, and we never used to use gloves. And I've got no cuts on my hands. *And*,' she says, 'I sure want to get these cuffs off.'"

"She really wanted to get those cuffs off." Kasamani laughed.

"'*And*,' she says," Mlongo repeated, "I sure want to get these cuffs off."

"She was trained before we had all these rules about wearing gloves to examine patients," Hellen said.

"And she had no cuts on her hands," KK said. Savoring every line, every word.

"That Daktari, I tell you," said Mlongo as they all laughed in celebration of Linda and Mlongo's liberation. "She just wanted those cuffs off."

"But you're still in that house with the dead bodies," Prof G reminded Mlongo. "So how did you get out?"

"Oh sure, Prof, we were still in the house. We could either wait there until we were recaptured, or start walking west toward Kenya—and get recaptured on the road. But after being in that house all night, we decided we'd rather risk being recaptured on the road, so we just started walking."

"You just walked away."

"We just took those chains off and walked away."

"And you didn't pick up those AKs so you'd have some protection?" Kasamani asked.

"Didn't even think of it," Mlongo admitted, and he started laughing again. "Can you imagine Daktari with an AK?"

"So," Prof continued, "you walked all the way to Liboi?"

"By the way, Prof, I think we would have done that, but this *mzee* with a red beard driving a pickup stopped and told us to get in the back."

"So you just got in?" asked Hellen. "You got yourselves kidnapped again?"

"I thought so," Mlongo confessed. "Especially as the *kijana* in the front with the driver had an AK."

"You got into *that* vehicle?" asked Kasamani. "You got yourself captured again?"

"Hey, Kas, I don't argue with an AK. The man with the gun says get in, I get in!"

"No," said KK, "you don't argue with an AK."

"And you still didn't know if you were being kidnapped again," said Prof.

"Still didn't know!" said Mlongo. "Still didn't know until the pickup stopped, and Bwana AK came back and pointed that thing at us and motioned us to get out, and then pointed down the road and said, 'Liboi.'"

"So you knew you were home," said KK.

"Oh no," said Mlongo, "Daktari is standing there, looking like we had only been moved and were going to be locked up again in the back of some house, and then I said, 'Liboi, *Kenya*'—and oh how Daktari was smiling then!"

"You said, 'Liboi, *Kenya*,' and that was all she needed," laughed Hellen.

"Now she knew she was back home," said Kasamani—and now they all laughed again, celebrating not only the liberation, but now the homecoming itself.

"She just wanted to get those cuffs off," said KK. And one more time, Mlongo told that part of the story, and they all laughed again when Linda ruffled through the dead man's pockets looking for keys, not worrying about AIDS because she was trained before anyone knew about it.

**3**

"What are you doing here, Linda?" She knew the voice well, but from where? The hospital? Church? She turned, scanning the crowd: several hundred people on the grounds of a school, right next to a church. "I'm here, Linda," and just behind her she found Mlongo, dressed casually, carrying an infant and holding the hand of a small child. She hadn't seen him for several months.

"What are *you* doing here?" she countered. "You don't seem like the type to spend the day at a church choir competition."

"I don't?" he asked, grinning. "What is the type that spends a day at a church choir competition?"

"Well…I don't know!" She laughed. "I just didn't think it would be your type. But I guess it wouldn't be my type either!"

"So what brings you here? I've never seen you at these before."

"The simple answer is that Mercy used to sing in these competitions every year—Mercy is the one who used to work for me, but died last year…"

"Yes, yes, I remember. The one who had eclampsia."

"Exactly. And this will be the first competition in a long time with her not singing. I've never come before, so I thought this would be a good way to remember her, to see what was so important to her." She smiled. "So what's your excuse?"

"Well, Linda. I have no excuse!" He laughed again. "Our family comes here every year, for so many years now. Monica sings in our church choir—probably the best alto there—and I wouldn't miss this competition for anything. Of course I like it when her choir wins, but (and don't tell her this!) I really just love hearing *all* the choirs."

"Yeah, it sure isn't disco music."

"Oh, disco is good too, but this stuff…wow! By the way, I don't guess you've met Gift yet. This is our latest, born just four months ago."

"Gift? You mean Zawadi?" She reached up to grasp the baby's hand.

"No, no. Gift. We're Us Guys, remember? Her name is Gift."

"I actually haven't really met any of your kids; I only saw them from a distance when we were welcomed with that red carpet after we came back from Somalia."

"Oh, that's terrible. Well, this one here is Precious"—Linda reached down and shook his hand—"and Monica has the first two with her, that is Destiny and George. I think she is warming up somewhere with her choir. So, how have things been with you?"

"That's a good question. I haven't thought about it much, but I think I've been more tired since the, um, red carpet treatment. I haven't been sleeping well. Maybe that's it."

Mlongo nodded. "Yeah, sometimes I go right to sleep, then wake up for no reason."

"I imagine psychiatrists would enjoy telling us what all this means…"

"And relieving us of quite a few shillings…"

"And giving us sleeping pills. But I don't want sleeping pills that will make me groggy the next day. There's too much going on. At the end of this year MSF says they will be leaving the District Hospital. Their official line is that by then capacity will have been built and it will be sustainable. But everybody knows that as soon as they go things will be back to where they were—only worse, because they raised the expectations of everyone, and called it raising the standard, and there's no way that will continue. Funny thing is, they know all this. Even Gillian, bless her heart: she is rightly proud of what they've done, but even she admits things will fall apart. But she can't help it, poor girl. She's so passionate, and just can't help offering what she sees is the best."

Mlongo nodded, his smile tinged with sadness. "I know her very well. You are exactly right. But for now, isn't it good that people are getting decent care?"

"Yes, for *now*, but—"

"What is it someone said once, that *wazungu* are 'greedy for the future.' What's wrong with decent care for now?"

"Mlongo, I thought you were one of Us Guys! You're starting to sound like a village politician."

"Ah, Linda." Mlongo smiled. "You are treating Us Guys like we are *wazungu*. We're not—we're just Us Guys."

Linda nodded her "Yup, missed it again" nod, one she found herself using more and more, and looked down as Precious started pulling on his father's hand.

"What is it, Precious? Yes, yes, you can go and play with Ericki. Yes, go ahead."

"So it looks to me like Gift never cries," Linda said.

"Oh, Gift knows very well how to cry, especially when no one is around. She likes people—so all these people just make her happy."

"She takes after her dad, I see. And speaking of her dad, how are you doing? I hear the AIDS Institute has really expanded, and you keep climbing. Have you reached the top?"

Now Gift started to fuss, and Mlongo jiggled her. "Yes, the AIDS Institute is growing very big—but no, I will never reach the top. The top is…well, the top is where the money comes from, and that is not here." He shifted Gift to the other hip and gave a sardonic smile, one Linda hadn't seen before. "Have you heard the Institute is changing its name? They've got this international reputation and they want to build on it, so they are still calling it the AIDS Institute—but now AIDS has two meanings: the disease of course, but now also African Innovations in Data Synergies. They—or I should say we—have become the real Kenyan center for the NMPSP, and Hodges is still carrying on about how the AIDS part is still the center and I should still be the director there. But…"

Linda waited. Then: "So are you still the director of the AIDS part?"

"As of now, yes."

"As of now? What does that mean?"

"Well, OK, so I've started getting really interested in research. The problem is, some of the most interesting and important questions are either not answered, or are dealt with superficially by graduate students who hardly ever get funded. So, Prof and Hellen and KK have been working to set up this Research Center with the consortium where *they*—that is, the faculty at the School of Medicine—develop the research agenda, and then consortium members help by either using their contacts to get money that is available, or even to influence the donors to offer money for the right questions. Well, OK, what *we* think are the right questions."

"So you're saying even research is donor driven?"

"You didn't know that? Oh, yes."

"So, have you moved to the university?"

"No, I'm still with the Institute—but I do admit that I have thought about applying to the School of Medicine. Well, actually I *have* applied, but that is not public knowledge yet."

"Wow! You've spent all those years working with NGOs—efficient, well-financed NGOs—and now you are thinking of moving over to a public university…"

"Yes. Which is far more inefficient, and subject to budget cuts and corruption and…I know, I know. It will be a switch. But Prof G says that my experience dealing with NGOs will be valuable as the university starts dealing with more and more American universities—and sure, that is work I don't mind and can do well. But what gets very tiresome is realizing that… well, that I'm Hodges's puppet. He gave me a lot of space when I just started there, but with all these NMPSP activities—and all the money that goes with them—he seems very, you know, involved. And during our little trip to Somalia? It seems that was his chance to…"

"Get back in the driver's seat?" Linda suggested.

Mlongo was about to answer when Monica walked up with the three older children. "Linda! I haven't seen you since that day you guys were ushered into the AIDS Institute…"

"…across a red carpet," said Mlongo.

"Yes, across a red carpet, and then all those photographers were there, and the choirs." She laughed. "We never had a chance to talk much, but I feel like I already know you. Leonard has told me some of what happened with both of you there."

Linda shook her hand warmly. "It seems I already know you too. And now your children—and my goodness, this small one is so good!"

"She really likes her daddy. She's not usually that quiet with me. Well, maybe that's because she knows I have something for her that her daddy doesn't." And they all laughed. "Mlongo, we start to sing in about fifteen minutes, so I brought these children back."

"No problem. We'll be listening." And together with the children, Linda and Mlongo moved toward the church where Monica's choir would be performing.

"By the way," Mlongo said as they walked, "even though I'm not at the university yet, they've put me on a committee. Prof G is interested in our NMPSP findings, and has asked the dean to think of starting general practice postgraduate training for doctors—so I'm on the Family Medicine Exploration Committee."

"Family practice, here in Kenya?" Linda asked.

"Yes, apparently under the consortium one of the universities—Wisconsin, I think—has some ideas and some resources to get it started."

"But what does family practice have to do with Kenya?"

"What do you mean?"

"Well, I trained in family practice—OK, it was many years ago, but I don't think things have changed a lot. And the patients we saw were people with diabetes and hypertension and obesity and depression—and colds! My goodness, they all came when they had a simple cold! That work is nothing like what I do here."

"OK," Mlongo said, "but the screening is telling us that at least some of the diseases on your list are here: the diabetes, hypertension, heart disease, cancer…"

"Fine, your screening says they are around. But *I'm* not seeing them very much at the District. Maybe St. Anthony's is seeing this 'epidemiological transition' that people talk about…in fact, maybe *only* St. Anthony's and other private hospitals are really seeing it. I guess you have to be rich to get these diseases." Linda paused. Then she said, "Wisconsin. Did you say Wisconsin? Isn't that where Walt is?"

"Yes, that's right. You know him, don't you?"

"Oh, yes."

"Prof was talking about how we need better-trained generalist doctors in Kenya, and Walt says family medicine is the way to go—adapted to our situation here, of course."

"OK, I think more training for medical officers would be useful…but why Walt? Why don't you guys just set up the training program yourselves?"

"Resources. Wisconsin and the other consortium members have resources: faculty exchange programs, fellowships, learning materials—and money. It takes a lot of people, energy, and money to set up a new program."

"Yes, and Walt sure has energy. But does he really know what we need here?"

"No, he probably doesn't." Mlongo stopped, then turned to Linda. "But you do. In fact, you were wondering what would happen to you at the District after MSF leaves. Why don't you apply to the university? Why don't you come and help us develop family medicine for Kenya?"

Linda laughed. "Me? I'm just a clinician, not an academic. Work at the university—and then have to deal with Walt all the time? Me?" And then Linda was really laughing.

They had arrived at the church. Monica's choir, in two-toned blue choir robes, was standing at the front, and the director was giving them a few last instructions, singing the opening line in tenor and bass, and then in falsetto soprano and alto. He raised his arms, sang the first few notes, and the tenors began.

*Alfajiri ya kupendenza, ni siku njema siku yenye baraka*
Dawn, pleasing dawn, a good day of blessing

Then the rest of the choir joined in full harmony:

*Jua imekwisha chomoza wamchao wote waliolala*
*Ndege nao wanalialia kumshukuru muumba*
The sun has already burst forth to waken the sleepers
And the birds sing thanks to their creator

By the third line the audience was beginning to join in.

*Njoni baba, mama na watoto, njoni wote mbele za*
*Bwana,*
*Tumtolee shukrani zetu kwakutoa sadaka*
Come, father, mother, and children, come all in front of the Lord,
We'll present our offerings of thanks

And by the end of the second time through the chorus everyone in the audience was standing. Linda took Precious and George with her to the aisle so they all could see better. The choir was accompanied by a keyboard, drums, and other percussion instruments that the choir members themselves played:

tambourines, *kayambas*, a Bic pen rubbed on the side of a ribbed Fanta bottle, and one tall fellow near the back was striking a metal rod inside a metal ring.

After the first verse, the tall fellow came out beside the choir and bent at the waist as he danced. From somewhere in the audience a small boy ran up to the drummer, and the tenor standing next to the drummer lifted the small boy onto a chair as he continued singing. Without missing a beat, the boy's father took his son's hands into his own and together they drummed, accompanying the celebration.

> The birds give thanks
> with their pleasing voices,
> And we give thanks
> for the gifts we've been given…

It was too good, too real to end after the third verse, so they kept going around. For ten or fifteen minutes they sang thanks; thanks no one wanted to stop giving. More than halfway through, George pulled on Linda's hand, pointing to the director. He had developed a small dance, with each beat spreading out one leg, returning it, spreading the other, returning it, all as he directed. The tall fellow banging the metal ring began to move toward the front of the choir, and as they came to the final time through the chorus, he faced the director and copied his dance steps perfectly, smiling seriously.

Finally, with an exaggerated ritardando of the entire last line, the song came to an end, and the whole audience erupted in applause. Linda made her way back to Mlongo with Precious and George in tow. Mlongo was still swaying slightly, as if the music continued in his head, with Destiny at his side, Gift in his arms, and tears in his eyes.